The Doll Hospital

James Duffy

Look for these and
other Apple paperbacks
in your local bookstore!

The Bears Upstairs
by Dorothy Haas

Me and Katie (The Pest)
by Ann M. Martin

Margaret's Moves
by Berniece Rabe

Veronica the Show-off
by Nancy K. Robinson

The Cats Nobody Wanted
by Harriet May Savitz

When the Dolls Woke
by Marjorie Filley Stover

The Doll Hospital

James Duffy

Interior illustrations
by Susan Tang

AN
APPLE
PAPERBACK

SCHOLASTIC INC.
New York Toronto London Auckland Sydney

ISBN 0-590-41855-6

12 11 10 9 8 7 6 5 4 3 2 1   2   0 1 2 3 4 5/9

Printed in the U.S.A.   28

For Annie and Pip

Chapter One

Alison sat patiently on Dr. Long's steel table while he listened to her heart, back and front. The table was cold under her bare legs. She knew what Dr. Long was going to do next. He pressed under her ears, then under her arms. It hurt the way it did sometimes, and, in spite of herself, she jumped. Dr. Long made a face, then he smiled. "I'm sorry, Alison. I always do that, don't I? Now, let's take a look at your throat."

Alison put her head back and opened her mouth wide. Dr. Long pulled out his little flashlight and unwrapped the flat piece of wood he used to hold her tongue down. He peered deep inside her mouth. "Well, that's okay," he said.

"I suppose you want another one of these tongue depressors?"

Alison nodded. Nettie would be upset if she didn't get *her* piece of wood. She took the little package. "Thank you, Dr. Long."

"Now, let's see about your weight," Dr. Long said. He helped Alison down from the table onto the scales. He fiddled with some knobs until the red numbers stopped flashing. He made another face and fiddled with them some more.

"You are going to have to drink more milk shakes, Alison. Maybe your mother can mix up an egg in them."

"I don't like milk shakes much anymore," Alison said. "I'll eat the egg plain, if that's all right."

"You can bet it's all right. How do you like your eggs best, Alison?"

"Soft-boiled, that's how my mother says they are best for me. I don't care much." She picked Nettie off her pile of clothes and gave her to her mother to hold along with the little package. She knew what Dr. Long was going to say next, it was the same thing he always said.

As she slipped into her shoes, she heard him. "Why don't you wait outside a minute, Alison, while I talk with your mother? She will only be a minute. I'll see you next month." He patted her on the shoulder, guiding her toward the door.

"I have to get my doll," Alison said. She took Nettie from her mother and walked very carefully into the waiting room. The woman at the desk put her hand over the telephone and smiled. "Your mother will be right out, Alison. Why don't you take a seat?" She went back to talking on the phone.

How did she know my name? Alison wondered. There was always a different woman in Dr. Long's office. It was strange that they all seemed to know her name. "But they don't know your name, do they, Nettie?" she whispered to her doll. "They don't even ask." Once, in the hospital, Dr. Long had said, "So this is Nettie, is it? That's a nice name for a doll."

But he never spoke to Nettie again. Nettie's feelings were hurt. "I don't think much of Dr. Long," she told Alison.

Alison hugged Nettie close and leaned back into the corner of the uncomfortable bench. She was tired. The visits to Dr. Long always made her very tired. She felt the throbbing of the blood through her veins — or was it arteries? She began to feel dizzy.

Nettie complained a little, the way she did when they went to see Dr. Long. "I don't like

it here, Alison. Why don't we go home?"

"Shhh, Nettie," Alison whispered. "We'll be home soon. Then we can talk. Look, I got you a tongue thing. Be patient, Nettie."

Alison shut her eyes and took a deep breath. Slowly she let it out, just as the nurses in the hospital taught her. Her legs felt heavy. She wouldn't be able to move them now. Mama and the woman would have to help her to the car.

When they got home, Christopher would be there to take her down the hall to her room, which used to be her father's study. "If I'm going to be a doctor, I have to learn how to help sick people move around," he told Alison. In the hospital it was mostly Christopher who stayed with her. Mama always started to cry and had to leave the room. Christopher stayed. He was thirteen, almost fourteen, and didn't ever cry. He read to her and teased her and helped the nurse give the medicine. He talked to Nettie and Boodles like they were sick and he was the doctor.

Mama came out of Dr. Long's office. She was tucking a Kleenex into her bag. She held out her hand. "Can we make it today, Alison?"

Alison stood up. Her legs wouldn't work. Her head went around like a top. Mama took her by one arm and the woman whose name she didn't know took her other arm.

"Shall I take your doll?" the woman asked.

"No!" Alison almost shouted. She didn't feel well, but she could still hold Nettie. "I mean, no, thank you. She's all right. I have her."

It was Dad, not Christopher, who came to the car when Mama blew the horn. "I came home early to see my princess," he smiled. "How is Her Highness today? And how is Princess Nettie?"

Alison tried to smile. Dad was always fooling around, but you could see he wasn't laughing, really. He gave a quick look over Alison's head to her mother, who, Alison sensed, shook her head. That's what always happened when Dad was there to meet them.

"Well, Princess, it's back to your boudoir." Dad picked her up, rubbed her ear with his nose, and carried her down to his old study. He laid her on the bed, took off her shoes, and pulled the summer quilt up over her. "I'll go see what the queen is fixing for supper. You rest for a while, Princess."

"Dad," Alison asked. "Where is Christopher?"

"Christopher has a paper route now. He delivers the afternoon paper."

"He didn't tell me about it."

"That's because he didn't know. He's just taken over Mark's route. He called me at the office to say he would be late."

"That's nice," Alison murmured. "Christopher needs to get out into the fresh air, doesn't he, Nettie?"

"I'm going to make him take me along some afternoon," Nettie said. "I need fresh air, too."

Alison scarcely heard her, as she drifted into sleep.

Chapter Two

Alison awoke to the sounds of her parents talking. In the corner of her room the soft pink light next to Dad's books was on. She heard a squeak upstairs in Christopher's room, which was over the study that wasn't a study anymore. Christopher was leaning back in the old office chair Dad had given him. Once in a while he would lean back too far and the chair would tip over and Mama would rush up the steps to tell Christopher to be quiet, his sister was resting.

She sipped the juice from the glass beside her bed. It was warm. She took a small bite of the sandwich. It was that awful brown bread with peanut butter that Mama had ground up with

7

raisins. She put it back on her plate and listened to the murmur of voices in the living room down at the end of the hall. Dad had left the hall door cracked so they could hear her if she called for something.

Nettie was sound asleep. She was snoring just a little bit. Alison sat up and swung her legs over the side of her bed. The throbbing had gone away and her legs weren't so heavy. She slipped her feet into the bunny slippers Dad had brought her from Boston. She felt a chill across her shoulders. She took the fluffy blue bathrobe from the bedpost and put it on.

Alison crept down the hall toward the murmur of voices, which became words she could understand. A sliver of light slipped through the cracked door. Alison sat down behind the door, beyond the light. She leaned against the wall and listened. Someday Mama or Dad would catch her there, she supposed. She couldn't move very fast, that was for sure. Usually she could figure out when the talk was over. Mama would start to cry. Alison would hear Dad get up from his chair and go over to the sofa where Mama was. If she peeked, she could see him put his arm around Mama and hug her. It was time then for her to go back to her room. Pretty soon Mama or Dad would come down the hall to feel her forehead and take away the glass and plate.

Alison listened carefully. When Nettie didn't come with her, she had to tell Nettie what was going on later. If she didn't, Nettie would sulk and tell Alison that she didn't like her anymore. Then Alison had to hug her and promise not to leave her behind the next time.

"It's not working," she heard her mother say. "Dr. Long can't be certain yet, but he doesn't think it's working. She's lost another pound-and-a-half. And the count isn't going up. And she's weak, Ted. She's, oh, so weak. We almost had to carry her out to the car. She can't go back to school next month. It's impossible."

"We'll see," Dad said. "Remember last year this time, we were sure she wouldn't get back to school. And she did."

"Some of the time she did, you mean. Some of the time she didn't. And she didn't finish. She went into the hospital again in April."

Alison wondered why Mama never used her name. It sounded as though she was talking about someone else, someone named She. Some night, Alison thought, some night I'm going straight out into the living room and say, "Mama, my name's not She. My name's Alison, Alison Jennifer Taggert. You can call me Princess, like Dad does, but not She." She would ask Nettie what she should do. Nettie would tell her.

Mama was talking again. "She's only eight, Ted, only eight years old. I can't accept it. There's something wrong. There's something awfully wrong when a little eight-year-old girl is sick like this, and they can't do anything about it. I can't accept that. I've tried, but I can't accept it."

"We just have to wait," Dad said. "Dr. Long is the best doctor there is. He's in touch with other specialists up in Boston. We have to trust him. He says they are on the edge of a breakthrough for cases like this."

That was a new word for Nettie, "breakthrough." Alison was pleased. Nettie would want to know what that meant. She stood up to creep back to her room. And stopped. Mama was talking some more. Alison peeked through the crack. Dad was still in his chair, and Mama was leaning forward on the sofa, her arms crossed. Her face was red. Pretty soon she'd start crying. Alison decided to wait.

"What he said was," Dad went on, "they have a new drug they haven't tested too much yet. In some cases the results are extremely encouraging. It's experimental."

Alison was interested. This was a lot better than most of the talk she heard at night. "Tests" she knew all about. They were always testing her. "Experimental" was something else. What did that mean? She would have to make something up for Nettie. Or maybe she could save it until she asked Christopher. That's what she'd do, she'd ask Christopher before she told Nettie and Boodles about the new word.

Dad was still talking. "Dr. Long told us he can get it, Martha, you know that. But we have to decide if we want him to use it."

"Alison isn't a guinea pig. She's only a baby. How can we decide? We don't know."

Mama had used her name. Alison was happy. Mama said she was her baby and her name was Alison, just like Nettie was her baby, although her name wasn't always Nettie. When she was new, she had another name, which Alison couldn't remember any longer. Nettie didn't like it, she told Alison. She was Nettie now and Nettie she was going to stay.

"We may have to decide pretty soon, Martha. Dr. Long says there's a waiting list. And there will be papers for us to sign."

Now Mama began to cry. "I can't understand it. What's he saying, Ted? That it's all right to go ahead, that the papers will make it all right

11

if it doesn't work? I don't think I can sign those papers, Ted."

Alison heard Dad get up to go over to the sofa. It was time to go back to her room and wake Nettie to tell her what was going on. She really had something to tell Nettie tonight.

Chapter Three

In her bed Alison was suddenly exhausted. She felt all right, but she was so tired she could scarcely move. She took a sip of juice and shut her eyes. Nettie asked what happened in a sleepy voice. "Something pretty interesting. I'll tell you tomorrow," Alison answered and fell into a deep sleep. She did not hear her father tiptoe into the room to open the window and take the glass and plate away.

Nettie always awoke as soon as the first morning light began to fill the room. "Hey," she said, pulling at Alison's shirt sleeve. "Look at you. You went to sleep in your clothes. You went down the hall again last night and listened. You didn't even get into your pajamas."

Alison pushed the covers back. Nettie was right, she *was* still in her clothes. I must have been really tired, she thought. I guess I better change them now. She put her legs over the edge.

"Wait a minute," Nettie said. "You promised to tell me what they said."

"I know I did," Alison answered, "but I can't right now. I have to ask Christopher something. Dad used words I didn't understand; big words, the kind you like, Nettie."

She slipped out of her clothes and put on her pajamas, which had been hanging at the foot of the bed. Then she pushed her pillow against the back of the bed and sat up. In the mornings she felt pretty good. It was during the day that her head began to ache and she felt tired and sore all over.

"Words like what?" Nettie demanded impatiently. "Maybe I can tell you what they mean. I know a lot of big words."

"One of them was 'breakthrough' and the other was 'experi-something.' Now you be quiet for a minute. I have to look at your throat. Where did you put that thing Dr. Long gave me?"

Nettie reached under her pillow. She gave Alison the depressor. "Not so hard this time. Yesterday you choked me." She climbed on Alison's stomach and opened her mouth.

Alison took her Mickey Mouse flashlight from the drawer of the bedside table. She stuck the depressor and the light into Nettie's mouth. She looked inside. "You're okay, Nettie. Let's see how much you weigh." She lifted Nettie up and put her down. "Hmmm. I think you've lost some weight. We'll have to build you up. Promise to eat your peanut butter, Nettie, and I'll tell you a story."

"About ghosts?" Nettie asked.

"I guess so. But I've almost run out of ghost stories. You will have to think of something else you like next time."

It was exactly seven-thirty when Christopher tapped on her door and brought Alison's breakfast tray in, as he did every morning.

"Good morning, Alison," he said. "Today you get oatmeal with honey and worms, a soft-boiled shark's egg, and brown toast with mustard. Breakfast for a princess. And a lemon lollipop for Nettie. What do you say to that, Nettie?"

Nettie didn't answer. She pulled at Alison's sleeve. "Where's Boodles?" she whispered. "Tell him to find Boodles."

"Christopher," Alison said. "Do you see Boodles anywhere? He wasn't in bed last night."

Christopher knelt down. He pulled a ragged puppy out from under the bed. "He likes to sleep under the bed more than on top of the bed,

Nettie knows that." He brushed a dustball from Boodles's ear and put him down beside Nettie.

The doll pulled at Alison's sleeve again. "The words," she whispered. "The two big words."

Alison tried to remember the two words she had told Nettie when she woke up. It was hard to remember sometimes. "Christopher, what does 'breakthrough' mean and 'experi-something or the other'?"

"Experimental?"

"Yes, I think that's it, 'experimental.' "

"Well, 'breakthrough' means a discovery of something pretty important. 'Experimental,' that means something you're trying for the first time. Where did you hear those words?"

Alison couldn't tell Christopher she was spying on Mama and Dad. "I don't know," she replied. "Probably on the radio. I hear lots of words I don't know. Nettie always wants to find out what they mean."

"I'll see you two later," Christopher said. "I'm going downtown with Dad. Be sure to eat all your breakfast. Oh, I almost forgot. I'll be right back. I have a surprise."

Alison liked surprises. Christopher brought her things wrapped in funny shapes so you couldn't guess what was inside, things like a paper airplane he made in school you could throw across the room or a piece of pretty ribbon for Nettie's hair.

This time it was a big surprise. It was in a plastic bag. Alison could feel Nettie tremble with excitement. She put her hand into the bag. She felt a round head and hair that reached way down, clothes all the way to the feet, and shoes with buttons on the feet. It was a doll.

"Look, Nettie," Alison cried. She pulled an elegant doll from the bag. "Oh, Nettie, isn't she beautiful? Have you ever seen a doll like her? Where did you get her, Christopher?"

"Mark gave her to me for you. She is sort of payment for taking over his paper route, I guess. She's a French doll that belonged to Mark's big sister, but she never played with her, and now she's grown up. She said Mark could give it to you. The doll's name is — "

"Denise, I know it's Denise," Alison interrupted. "That's the name of a French doll I saw on television once."

"Well, you might as well call her Denise if you want," Christopher said. "It's a pretty good name. What do you say, Nettie?"

Nettie didn't say anything. She was staring hard at Denise. Her eyes burned with jealousy.

17

Chapter Four

Alison put Denise next to her pillow while she ate breakfast. She chattered to her, asking her all sorts of questions about what she liked to wear and how she did her hair and what her favorite color was. Denise did not answer. Alison offered her a spoonful of oatmeal. Denise turned her head away. When she finished, Alison pushed the tray to one side and held Denise on her stomach. "Why don't you talk to me, Denise?" she asked. Denise lowered her eyes and shook her head. She was embarrassed, Alison could see that.

Nettie and Boodles watched from the bottom of the bed, whispering to each other. Nettie smiled when Denise wouldn't talk. Boodles nodded his head. The two of them were up to something, that was clear. Nettie would tell her sooner or later. She couldn't ever keep a secret. Alison made a place for Denise at her side and shut her eyes. She felt happy but tired.

In a little while, her mother came into the room to straighten up. She helped Alison out of bed and into the bathroom. Then she made up the bed. She lined Nettie, Boodles, and Denise against the footboard.

Alison heard the dolls start to whisper. She looked up at Mama to see if she heard. Her mother wasn't paying any attention. She was looking toward the sewing room next to the study. "That room's a mess," she said half to herself. "I don't sew anymore, and I do my ironing in the kitchen. I wonder what we can use it for?"

She smoothed Alison's pillow. "You rest for a while, Alison. I'll bring you some ginger ale in a little while when you take your pill."

"Could I have root beer today, Mama?" Alison asked.

"If there is any, you can have it. How come, Nettie doesn't like ginger ale?" her mother teased.

"She does, really," Alison answered, "but she

gets tired of it, she says. Nettie is sort of finicky about things sometimes, don't you think, Mama? I hope Denise isn't that way."

As soon as Alison's mother left the room, Nettie was up beside her. "I'm not at all finicky," she said. "I just don't like ginger ale."

Alison imitated Nettie's squeaky voice, "And you certainly don't like oatmeal. Every morning when Christopher brings my tray, you disappear under the covers. Also, you don't like soft-boiled eggs."

"That's about all," Nettie protested. "I like everything else, don't I?"

"The trouble is there isn't a lot of everything else," Alison remarked. "I hope Denise won't be such a picky eater."

Nettie smiled, "Not for a while she won't," she said mysteriously.

"What do you mean, Nettie?"

"She won't be eating much for a while, that's what I mean."

Alison remembered Denise's turning her head away from the oatmeal.

"Why not? What do you know about how Denise eats?" she asked Nettie.

Nettie turned up her nose. "Only what Boodles tells me."

"Don't you tease me, Nettie. Dr. Long said I wasn't to get upset. It isn't good for me. What does Boodles know about Denise?"

"You'll have to ask him. I'm not teasing you. Boodles knows everything about Denise."

"How come he's so smart? Sometimes I don't think Boodles knows what's going on. He spends all his time sleeping under my bed."

"Oh, Boodles knows all right, don't you, Boodles? Come on up here and tell Alison what you know."

Boodles crawled up the length of the bed and flopped down between Nettie and Alison.

"What is it you know, Boodles?" Alison asked.

Boodles looked at Nettie.

"Go on and tell Alison what Denise said," Nettie ordered.

"Well," Boodles said shyly. "Denise said she was ill."

"What's wrong with her?" Alison asked. "She didn't look sick to me at breakfast time."

"Boodles doesn't know what it is," Nettie interrupted, "but Denise says it is contagious."

" 'Contagious,' what does that mean?"

"I don't know. Do you know, Boodles?" Nettie poked Boodles, who had already shut his eyes.

"Denise said it is something you catch from someone who is sick. She's afraid you or Nettie or I will get it."

"Who did she get whatever it is from?" Alison asked. "I really don't understand."

"Denise said she got it from Mark's little sister who was playing with her before she came here to live. She didn't like Denise so she gave her what she had."

"Why didn't she tell me?" Alison asked. "She could have told me about it this morning and I would have told Mama and we could have given her some pills to get well."

"She couldn't," Nettie said mysteriously.

Alison was really upset now. She was tired and wanted her morning nap. "Why not?" she demanded. "You two are hiding things from me. It's not fair. I don't keep secrets from you."

"Denise only speaks French," Boodles explained. "French and a couple of words in English. She can say 'good baby.'"

"Fiddlesticks. How do you know, Boodles? You don't speak French."

"But I understand it, and I do too speak a little," Boodles told Alison. "My mother was a French poodle. She spoke French to her children all the time."

Chapter Five

When Alison woke up, Boodles and Nettie were back at Denise's side. Denise was lying down. Alison sat up to see what was going on. Denise *did* look sick. She was very pale, and her eyes were closed. She was in one of Nettie's nightgowns, which was too small for her. Alison could see that Nettie and Boodles were worried. Nettie didn't seem to be jealous any longer.

"What are we going to do, Nettie? I can help you look after her a little, but Dr. Long said I have to rest most of the day. We'll talk to Christopher when he comes home."

"Denise has to have rest and quiet right now," Nettie answered. "Boodles says she has to have her own place because she's contagious."

24

"Christopher will know all about that. He's going to be a doctor. We'll have to wait."

"There's something we can do before then," Nettie said. She told Alison that Boodles and she had heard her mother talking about the sewing room. They could put Denise there. She and Boodles could look after her. Maybe they wouldn't catch whatever it was Denise had. Alison could help out whenever she was strong enough.

"But you have to get us into the sewing room," Nettie insisted. "That's important, isn't it, Boodles?"

Boodles nodded his shaggy head. Alison noticed there was still some dust stuck to his ear. She reached down to pick it off. "I'm going to have to give you a bath soon, unless you keep clean," she warned.

Alison thought about what to do. She could say she wanted to have a doll room to play in, but her mother wouldn't let her keep getting in and out of bed to play in the sewing room. And she *was* tired most of the time these days, especially after the treatments. More often than not she had to ring the bell to have her mother come help her into the bathroom. "What can I tell her, Nettie?" she asked.

"I'm thinking, too," Nettie said. "You could tell her Boodles and Denise and I need a room of our own, that we bother you when you want to go to sleep."

"That's a good idea," Alison said. She was pretty sure that Nettie's idea would convince her mother. She reached for the brass bell on the bedside table. She stopped. She had another idea.

"Listen, Nettie, you and Boodles take Denise into the sewing room. I am going to walk to the kitchen and ask Mama. She will give us the room then, I bet. Be careful with Denise. She looks pretty sick to me."

Alison got to her feet. After her nap she felt good. She started to shuffle down the hall. She paused. She lifted her left foot carefully, then put it down ahead of the other foot. She did the same with the right foot. She didn't have to shuffle, she discovered. Shuffling must have been just a habit. A step at a time, one hand on the wall, she walked the way she used to down the hall. Her head was a little dizzy, but she was used to that.

Mama was surprised to hear Alison, surprised and, Alison was sure, pleased. "Oh, it's you, darling, you startled me. It's been a while since you walked out here by yourself. Are you feeling better?"

Alison nodded and sat at the table. She watched her mother knead the dough for bread.

"Mama, may I ask you something?"

"What is it, Alison?" Her mother looked worried again and sat down on the other side of the table.

"Well," Alison began. "You know that sewing room next to the study? Could we make that into a place for Nettie and Denise and Boodles? There are three of them now, and they need a place of their own. Sometimes they talk a lot, and I can't rest the way I am supposed to. I'll still look after them, I promise."

"But Alison," her mother objected, just as Alison knew she would at first, "Dr. Long said you had to take it absolutely easy for a while so you will get well. Maybe later, when you are stronger. I'll move your friends into the sewing room if that's what you want, and bring them back whenever you ask for them."

Alison had her mind on the sick Denise. She needed rest and quiet, too. "Please, Mama, they are already in there. Maybe you could make just a little more room for them and hang up some of the things in there. That's all they need."

Her mother looked at Alison closely. She looked more worried now. "What are you up to, Alison? You're not supposed to do anything active."

Alison didn't like to cry unless she felt really bad, but she *had* to have the sewing room. She couldn't stop a few tears trickling down. "Please, Mama, please," she begged.

Her tears worked.

"I don't understand what you are doing, Alison, but if it means so much to you, I guess it's all right. You have to promise you are not going to run back and forth."

"I promise, Mama. Thank you." She stood up. She was wobbly and held onto the chair.

"You have overdone it, baby," her mother said. She gave Alison her arm for support. As they walked past the sewing room, they stopped to look inside. Denise was lying in a pile of folded curtains. Boodles was on one side, Nettie on the other.

"Don't you want Nettie with you, Alison? She's never been by herself. I don't know about that silly Boodles. I never see him unless I run the vacuum cleaner under the bed."

"Nettie will come back to me, Mama," Alison said. She didn't tell her mother Nettie could get back by herself. "It's just that they have to baby themselves every once in a while the way I do."

Her mother shook her head. "I still don't understand. Maybe I will someday. Into bed, Alison. I'll bring you lunch in half an hour."

Chapter Six

Alison was worn out from her morning's activities. She had not been so busy since she came home from the hospital. She did not hear her mother come into the room with a lunch tray and carry it away when she saw that Alison was asleep. She did not hear her mother rustling around in the sewing room. She did not hear Nettie tiptoe later to the bathroom and tiptoe out with a cup of water for Denise.

When she woke later in the afternoon she felt as though she was burning up. Her pajama top was wet. The pillow was damp where her head had rested. Alison was frightened; her heart started beating furiously. She knew what to expect when her fever went up: a lot of awful pills almost every hour day and night and, maybe, if the fever didn't go down, a trip to the hospital.

She threw back the sheet and sat upright. She was about to call her mother when she realized her throat wasn't dry. She put her hand to her forehead. It wasn't hot. The room was hot, that was for sure, but she didn't have a fever. The throbbing died down. The sun slanted in through the window. She noticed that the window was closed. Her mother hadn't wanted to awaken her. The air in the room was hot and sticky.

Alison sank back with a big sigh of relief. Then she got out of bed and pushed the window open. She turned on the fan on Dad's desk. She stood for a moment in front of the moving air. That was close, she thought. Dr. Long had told Mama and Dad he thought it would be better not to have an air conditioner in her room. Maybe later, he had said, let's wait and see.

Denise! What about poor, sick Denise stretched out in her pile of folded-up curtains? Alison almost ran from her room into the sewing room. Then she stopped at the door, surprised and confused. It didn't look the same at all. The sewing machine had disappeared. The curtains and all of Mama's sewing stuff were gone. Alison's bassinet had been brought down from the attic. Next to it, against the wall, were a couple of wooden boxes Alison had never seen before. Big labels at the end told her one was an apple box, the other was a pear box.

But where was Denise? And Nettie? And Boodles? There wasn't a sign of them in the sewing room. What had Mama done with them? Had Mama put them back in her room and she hadn't seen them? She went back to her room and looked everywhere. She peeked under the bed. No Boodles there. No dolls, either. She returned to the sewing room to have a really good look.

"Ssst. Hey, Alison!"

That was Nettie's voice. Puzzled, Alison looked in the boxes and the bassinet. There was a clean baby sheet over the pad in the bassinet, a little pillow, and a flannel baby blanket folded at one end, but not a sign of Denise or Nettie.

"We're in here, Alison. We're in the closet."

Someone pushed the closet door open. It was Boodles. He was panting. It was as hot in the sewing room as it was in Dad's study. It smelled stuffy. Mama hadn't opened the window.

Alison knelt down at the closet. There were three pillows on the floor. Denise was lying without moving on the one in the middle. Nettie sat on the pillow beside her, fanning Denise with a piece of cardboard. She smiled up at Alison, but she looked worried.

Alison leaned forward to touch Denise's forehead. It was hot. Denise moaned a little. She did not open her eyes. Alison saw an empty paper cup on the floor. Nettie had been nursing Denise. "I'll get some fresh water," Alison said, "and see if I can find half an aspirin. You keep fanning. If you get tired, let Boodles have a turn."

On the top shelf of her bathroom cabinet, Alison felt for her aspirin bottle. She was not supposed to touch it ever, but half a baby aspirin wasn't going to hurt, she told herself. Mama gave her four or five at a time when her fever was up. She twisted off the cap and poured some pink tablets into her hand. She saw a half mixed in with the whole ones. She took it and pressed the top on and put the bottle back on the top shelf. After this, she would let Christopher take care of the medicine. She ran half a cup of water and headed back to the sewing room.

"I'll give Denise the aspirin," Nettie said. "Then you hold her up and give her the water. Boodles and I tried to give her a drink before, but we spilled most of it. Tell Denise to open her mouth, Boodles."

Boodles said some funny sounding words to Denise. The doll opened her mouth. Nettie popped in the aspirin. Alison held Denise up and put the cup to her lips. Denise drank and drank and drank until the cup was empty. She smiled weakly, said something Alison didn't understand, and lay back on her pillow.

"What did she say, Boodles?" Alison wanted to know.

" 'Merci.' That means 'thank you.' "

"Ask her how she feels," Nettie ordered Boodles.

"I'll try," he said, "but I have forgotten most of my French." He said something else to Denise.

Denise half opened her eyes. She replied to Boodles and closed her eyes again.

"Well," Nettie said impatiently, when Boodles remained silent. "We can't wait all day. What did she say?"

"I think she said she was tired and wanted to sleep and please leave her for a while. She said, I think, that we shouldn't worry about her."

"Let's talk in a low voice," Alison said. "Why are you all in the closet, Nettie? Did Mama put you in here?"

"No, she put us each on a pillow on the floor, but the light hurt Denise's eyes, so we moved her into the closet. It was hot in there, but that was what she wanted."

"The closet is no good for someone who is sick," Alison said. "I can tell you that." She went to the window and pushed it open. She drew the shade down.

"I'm going to put her in the bassinet. I'll move a box right next to it, Nettie, so you can be close to her. What about you, Boodles? Are you going back under my bed or do you want to stay here?"

"I like the closet," Boodles said. "It's just as good as under your bed and not so dusty."

Alison lifted Denise tenderly and put her in the bassinet. Denise moaned again. "It's all right, Denise. In a little while you are going to get better. Nettie will be right here if you want something. We have to wait for Christopher. He'll tell us what to do next."

Chapter Seven

It was a hot day for delivering papers, Christopher told Alison. He sat in front of her fan drinking root beer. "What have you been up to, Alison?" he asked. "Mama says you went to the kitchen by yourself. That's pretty good. Did it wear you out?"

"A little," Alison admitted. "I slept all afternoon. When I woke up, I was so hot, I thought my fever had come back. It hadn't, though. But Denise is *really* sick."

"What's the matter with her?" Christopher looked around the room. "Where is she, anyway? And where is Nettie?"

"Close the door, Christopher. We have to talk about something."

35

After Christopher shut the door, Alison told him about the sewing room. She said Denise was ill with something contagious. Nettie and Boodles were nursing her. Denise had a high fever, Alison was certain. Alison and Nettie and Boodles had done everything they could, but Denise had to see a doctor.

"Will you please take a look at her, Christopher, and tell us what to do? They are waiting for you in the sewing room."

"They won't talk to me," Christopher said. "Nettie has never spoken to me. She only talks to you and you have to tell me what she says."

"That's because I'm always around," Alison told him. "Nettie is afraid you'll laugh at her if she talks to you. She says dolls aren't supposed to talk, except to each other, or to furries. That's why Boodles doesn't say anything, either."

"They are going to have to talk to me if they want my help," Christopher said. "They will have to tell me what's going on."

"I know," Alison agreed. "I have already told Nettie that. I am going to stay right here in my room. Then they will have to talk to you. Maybe not Denise. She only speaks French. But Boodles will tell you what she says. His mother was a French poodle."

"Okay, I'll try. An aspirin will probably help.

That's what Mama gives me. You, too, when you have a fever."

"I have already given her an aspirin." Alison said.

"You know you're not supposed to take medicine unless Mama gives it to you, Alison."

"It was only half an aspirin. I won't do it again."

Christopher went into the sewing room, closing the door behind him. Alison strained to hear what was going on. There were voices. It seemed to her she could hear Nettie and another deeper voice. It had to be Boodles. She smiled to herself. Now Christopher would believe her. She knew that he and Mama and Dad only pretended to agree when she told them what Nettie said or did. They didn't really believe Nettie could talk and move around like everybody else.

Christopher stayed in the sewing room a long time. Finally, he came out. "It's measles," he reported to Alison. Denise has spots on her back and her tummy. She'll probably have them on her face tomorrow."

He saw the fear in Alison's eyes. "It's not serious. They will go away after a while. Denise will be all right."

"You *are* a doctor, Christopher," Alison said. "I told Nettie you were a doctor; not like Dr.

Long — he's a specialist, Mama says — but a doctor anyway."

"You shouldn't tell Nettie things like that. I just do what I see Mama and Dad do when someone is sick."

"Then how did you know it was measles?"

"Easy enough. Mark told me his little sister Sandra had them. Denise said Sandra was playing with her before Mark gave her to you. Measles are — "

"Contagious," Alison almost shouted. "I told you that. It's a new word Boodles told me. Denise told him. She said Sandra made her sick on purpose."

"She didn't have to," Christopher said, "but maybe she did. Mark says Sandra is a mean little kid."

"What about Nettie?" Alison worried. "Will she get them?"

"Maybe not. Sometimes you don't get them. She told me she and Boodles could look after Denise most of the time."

"See, Christopher, she does talk. You didn't believe me, did you?"

"I sort of half did. I figured you couldn't make up everything you told me."

"Christopher, will you make a sign for the sewing room, a sign that says 'Hospital', and put it on the door? Just in case Nettie and Boodles get the measles. I'm going to be the nurse from now on; I'll tell Mama."

"I'll make the sign," Christopher agreed, "but I don't know about the nurse business. You know what Dr. Long said. And you don't want to worry Mama and Dad. You can't exert yourself."

"He said I should do what I felt like doing. I was the best judge of that, he said. When I'm tired, I will rest. I'll do everything I am supposed to do, I promise. You can tell Mama I'm hungry. I smelled something good when you opened the door. What was it?"

"Hamburger," Christopher said.

"Please tell Mama I want a big one."

Chapter Eight

Darkness settled in. A cooling breeze made the curtains move. Mama came to take the supper tray away. "You ate everything tonight, Alison. Good. The last time we had hamburger you hardly ate any at all. I'll turn the fan off when I go to bed," she said. "Now, you go to sleep. You had an active day."

"I was hungry," Alison replied. "Good night, Mama." She held out her arms to give her mother a hug and a kiss.

Her mother put the tray down and held Alison tight. She stroked Alison's hair down over the back of her neck. "I love you, I love you, I love you so much. You are always going to be my baby, Alison. You sleep well, and don't be afraid to ring the bell if you want something."

Alison stretched out under the sheet and closed her eyes. When she was sure that Mama would not return, she slipped into the sewing room. "Nettie, where are you?" she whispered. "Shall I turn on the light?"

"Over here beside the bassinet," Nettie said. "Be careful. We don't need a light. Denise is asleep."

Alison found the bassinet with her outstretched hand. She leaned over and listened. Denise was breathing normally, not short and fast the way she was breathing this afternoon when the fever was up. "Her fever has gone down," she told Nettie. "That's good. It was the aspirin."

"I felt her head," Nettie said. "She's not hot now. Boodles and I are taking turns. I am going to wake him up after a while and he will take over. You don't have to worry about us."

"I won't," Alison found herself saying. She realized she *did* trust Nettie and Boodles. They had watched Mama looking after her. Now they knew what to do. But that wouldn't leave much for Alison to do. I'll supervise, she thought, remembering the head nurse at the hospital. Christopher can be the doctor, and I'll be the head nurse. Nettie can be the night nurse. And Boodles? She couldn't see him as a regular nurse.

41

Boodles would be in charge of whatever came up. We will all work together, she decided, and make Denise well again.

"I am going to bed now," she told Nettie. "You be sure to wake me up if you need me."

"Get us a fresh cup of water first," Nurse Nettie said. "That's all we will need."

Alison brought the water to the sewing room. She put it on the floor under the bassinet. "It will be safe there. We'll get a table soon," she told Nettie. "Good night. Oh, Nettie, you're so good, I'm never going to part with you." She picked the doll up and hugged her tight, then put her down on the pillow.

She heard a familiar murmur of voices at the end of the hall. Alison was tired, but she thought she had better listen for a minute just to keep track of what was going on. She hunched down behind the door.

"What did Dr. Long say when you called him?" Dad asked.

"He said that happened sometimes. Sick children store their energy and are restless until they use it up. He didn't think it had any significance."

"Significance." That was a good word. Alison told herself she would have to remember that one. She sounded it out the way her teacher last year, Miss Harrison, had taught her. Sig-nif-i-cance. Tomorrow she'd ask Christopher what it meant.

For a minute she forgot the talk in the living room and thought about school. She was a little sad she wouldn't be going back. Still, school wasn't all that great when you had trouble holding your head up and you felt awful half the time. Sometimes she had to tell Miss Harrison to please call her mother to come and get her because she had to lie down.

But it was better than staying home all day. After a while, the cartoons on television were all the same. Her back ached just from being in bed. Dad's study wasn't the best room to be sick

43

in. Most of the year the sunshine never came in. Mama said she would redo the study if they could just move Alison out for a while, but Alison couldn't handle the steps up to her old room, so she stayed in the study.

Mama was talking again. "She did seem different today, Ted; not better, but different, not so quiet and far away from us. And not a single complaint, not one."

"You told the doctor?" Dad asked.

"Yes, I did. He said not to put too much stock in that. There would be changes from day to day. He didn't think one day's activities gave us much cause for encouragement. But for a while, Ted, today was just like the old days, before Alison was sick."

"Encouragement," that was another word for Christopher. The way Mama pronounced it made the word sound important. It was going to be a mouthful for Nettie.

"We asked him to be honest with us, Marty, you know we did. We have to know what's going on. We can't build on false hopes."

Alison was back in her room. She didn't hear what Dad was saying. Two good words were enough for one evening, and now she was really tired.

Chapter Nine

"I have been to see our patient, Nurse," Christopher told Alison. He handed her a glass of orange juice from the breakfast tray.

"How is Denise this morning?"

"She has no fever, but that's usual in the morning. She is still tired. The spots haven't spread to her face. Sometimes they don't, I guess."

"What did she say?" Alison asked.

"You know talking to Denise is a problem," Christopher explained. "If she is going to stay here, she will have to learn English. Boodles isn't that good at French, and it takes a long time while he thinks about what she has said. Maybe that's why Mark's sister never played with Denise. They couldn't understand each other."

"Maybe," Alison said. "Dolls don't talk to everyone, Christopher. It takes a lot of patience. They have to trust you first. You know how long it took before Nettie said anything."

"Well, she talks a mile a minute now. I couldn't get a word in yesterday, she was talking so much. She's sort of bossy, isn't she?"

"That's just Nettie's way," Alison said. "You will get used to it. I'll take that other piece of toast now, thank you. I think we should ask Nettie to teach Denise English. Boodles and I can help her. Dolls learn fast."

"How about you, Alison? Mama says you were busy all day yesterday. Do you feel okay this morning? No spots anywhere?" he teased.

"I'm all right. What they gave me at the hospital last time must be working. I have to go see Denise now. I'll get fresh water for her."

The door to the sewing room was closed. On the door was a piece of white cardboard. At the top Christopher had carefully printed with a Magic Marker:

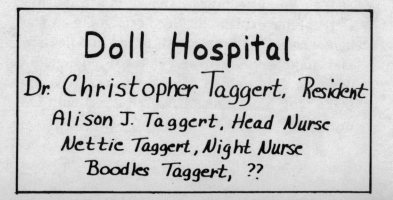

Doll Hospital
Dr. Christopher Taggert, Resident
Alison J. Taggert, Head Nurse
Nettie Taggert, Night Nurse
Boodles Taggert, ??

Denise was sitting up in her bassinet, the small pillow at her back. Nettie had brushed her dark hair and tied it with a white ribbon. She had on a pair of Nettie's pajamas. I'll have to ask Mama to make some more doll clothes, Alison thought. She can teach me how to sew and I'll help.

Denise smiled shyly at Alison. Her smile grew bigger when Christopher bent over to help her drink from the cup.

"*Merci, monsieur le Medicin*," she said.

"That's 'Thank you, Doctor,' isn't it?" Christopher said. "Now, Denise, say 'Thank you, Doctor.' "

Denise said slowly, "Thank you, Doctor."

"Very good," Christopher said. "Where is Nettie?"

Denise pointed to the apple box under the window. Nettie had put her pillow inside the box. She was curled up fast asleep.

"Where is Boodles?" Alison asked her.

Denise pointed to the closet. "Nettie tired, Boodles tired," she said.

"Denise tired, too," Christopher told her. "Sleep now."

Denise stretched out in the bassinet. She closed her eyes. Alison spread the flannel blanket over her. She remembered the words she had heard last night. She had better ask Christopher what they meant before he went off, so she could tell them to Nettie when she woke up.

"Come into my room," she whispered to Christopher. "I have some words for you. Could you get me a glass of ginger ale first, please?"

"Ginger ale?" Christopher said with surprise. "Mama said you didn't like ginger ale anymore."

"That was yesterday," Alison smiled. "Today I feel like ginger ale."

"If that's what you want, Princess, that's what you will have." Christopher came back with a tinkling glass of ginger ale. "It was warm. I put some ice in it. What are today's words? I have to cut the grass before it gets too hot outside."

"Sig-nif-i-cance. I think that's it."

"That means something important. What's the other one?"

"En-cour-age-ment, is that right?"

"Yes. That's a tough one. It means to kind of help someone do something by talking, like 'I encourage you to drink your ginger ale.' I would tell you it was good for you or something, understand?"

Alison nodded. She didn't really understand. She decided she might just tell Nettie the first word. She'd save the other one. She wondered what Dr. Long meant when he told Mama something wasn't much cause for encouragement. It didn't sound too good. She better take it easy today, she thought. She climbed under her sheet.

"Thank you, Christopher. If I am awake I want to go see Denise with you on your next call."

Chapter Ten

Alison decided to stay mostly in her bed for the next couple of days. She felt a little better than she had in quite a while, and she didn't want to push it. When her mother came to visit, she asked for a notepad and a pencil. "I have to make myself a schedule," she told her. "I am on duty in the hospital during the day. Nettie is the night nurse."

"I know," her mother said. "I saw the sign. The sewing room really does look like a hospital now. I am sure Denise is well attended to. What about poor Boodles? Doesn't he have a title?"

"Nettie and I are thinking about that. Nettie says he has a lot of responsibilities — is that the right word, Mama? — and he doesn't need a title."

"Yes, that is the right word. Nettie certainly has a large vocabulary these days. Do you teach her or does she pick the words up for herself?"

"Both," Alison said. "When Denise is better, we are going to learn French."

"What is the paper for?" her mother asked.

"Christopher said I should check on things about every three hours."

"You look after yourself at the same time, Alison. If you are asleep, I'll fill in for you. I am a pretty good nurse, too, you know." Her mother leaned over and kissed her. "I'll be upstairs if you want me. Ring the bell."

Alison nodded. She didn't plan to miss any of her rounds. Nettie wouldn't talk to Mama; at least she never had. Maybe someday, but not yet. Nettie probably wouldn't have talked to Christopher if Denise had not been sick. Alison settled back to think about the doll clothes Nettie and Denise needed. She kept one eye on the clock.

At eleven-thirty, Denise was sitting on a pillow beside her bassinet listening to Nettie read to her. She looked much better. There was a touch of red in her cheeks, and her eyes sparkled when she saw Alison.

"Good morning, Alison," she said very

slowly, but clearly. "How are you?"

Before Alison could reply, Boodles spoke up. "Very good, Denise. That was fine."

"It certainly was," Alison joined in. "What do *you* think, Nettie? We must give Denise some encouragement."

Nettie put down the book. "What does that mean?" she asked.

"It means we have to help Denise with her English," Alison said proudly.

"Humph," Nettie said. "I am already giving her encouragement. I am reading her a story. Boodles is explaining what she doesn't understand."

"Yes, Alison," Denise interrupted. "They are very good teachers. Is that right, Boodles, 'good teachers'?"

"Yes, indeed," Boodles said. "Teachers is a hard word. I am going to take my noontime nap now." He went into the closet and closed the door to a crack.

"I think I will rest, too," Nettie said. "After all, I am the night nurse. Please help Denise into bed before you leave." Nettie climbed into her box under the window. Alison drew the shade all the way down.

"Are you better today?" she whispered to Denise.

"I am much better, thank you," the French doll answered.

"You speak very well," Alison went on, trying not to use big words.

"No, but I am learning," Denise answered. "I heard English a lot, but I never speak until now."

"When you are well," Alison asked, "will you teach me French?"

Denise raised her eyebrows. "You want the French?" she asked, uncertain.

"Yes, I want to learn French."

"*Merveilleux! Le français, c'est une belle langue.* Do you understand?"

"Yes," Alison answered, "French . . . is . . . a . . . something language. Is that right?" She shook her head. "I do not understand *belle*."

"*Belle, belle,*" Denise repeated. She called into the closet. "Boodles, what is *belle*?"

"Beautiful. *Belle* means beautiful, I think."

"Yes," Denise said. "French is a beautiful language." She sighed and leaned back in her pillow.

"You are still sick, Denise," Alison said. "I'll help you into the bassinet." She lifted Denise and put her down gently in the bassinet. "Someday," she told her, "we'll take Nettie and go to France. Someday soon, maybe, as soon as I get well."

Chapter Eleven

Each day that passed, Denise was better. The spots paled, and her fever went away for good. On the fourth day she left the bassinet. "I will sleep on my pillow with Nettie and Boodles from now on," she told Christopher. "You can use the bassinet for someone else who is sick."

Nettie was feeling very proud of herself. "I am a pretty good nurse, wouldn't you say, Alison? Boodles and I pulled Denise through the measles, didn't we, Boodles?"

Boodles looked at Alison and smiled. "We had some help from Alison and Christopher, Nettie. You shouldn't forget them."

"That's true," said Nettie, "but we are only dolls. No one expects much from dolls — or furries. We aren't supposed to do significant things."

Alison laughed. "But you have to admit Christopher and I gave you a lot of encouragement."

Nettie didn't pay any attention. "Also," she went on, "we have taught Denise to speak English; haven't we, Denise?"

"Yes," Denise responded. "Now I must teach Alison how to speak French. She says she is going to take me back to Paris as soon as she is better."

"Back to Paris?" Boodles asked. "Do you mean that you are really French? You didn't tell me that. My mother is a French poodle, but I don't think she came from France."

"Oh, yes," Denise said. "I am not a French doll because I look French. Paris was my home when I was younger."

Nettie was astonished. She could hardly believe her ears. Her patient, Denise, it turned out, was not an ordinary patient. "That's even more significant," she told Alison. "Imagine an ordinary doll like me nursing a French princess."

"I am not a princess," Dense said. "I was very fancy, I believe, and ever so expensive, but not a princess. And, I forgot to tell you, Boodles, I won a prize."

Even Christopher, who had not been paying too much attention to doll talk, was interested.

"What kind of prize, Denise?"

"Well, every year they have a great big doll show in Paris. It is the largest doll show there is. Dolls come to Paris from all over the world."

"How about furries?" Boodles wanted to know. "Do they let stuffed dogs and bears and rabbits into the doll show?"

"I am sorry, Boodles, that the show is only for dolls. Furries probably have their own show somewhere else."

"Go on, Denise, tell us all about it." Alison was entranced. Imagine having such a famous doll in her own house. She picked Nettie up to hold in her lap. "Let Nurse Nettie hear all about her patient."

"Hundreds of dolls, maybe thousands, come to the doll show. They are put on exhibit."

"What does that mean?" Nettie asked.

"The dolls are dressed up in their finest clothes. Hairdressers prepare their hair. Some of them wear jewelry. They are put up on glass shelves in a big room for everyone to see. At the end of the show they select the best doll. They chose me. I don't know why, because there were other dolls who were more beautiful, and certainly there were more elegant dolls, but, to my surprise, they did select me."

"If you were so famous in Paris, why did you leave?" Christopher asked.

"Some very rich people bought me to be with their child in your country. They put me in a gold box and brought me here in an airplane.

"I am sorry to tell you that their daughter Patricia couldn't have me for her friend. Her mother was so proud of how much they paid for me, as if that made any difference, that she talked about nothing else. She told Patricia she had to be very careful with my clothes and hair. Poor Patricia only wanted to play with me, but she didn't dare. Finally she stood me on a shelf and forgot about me while she played with her old dolls. She didn't even give me a name.

"Patricia's mother was very disappointed. 'Well,' she said, 'if you aren't going to play with the expensive French doll we brought all the way from Paris, we will give her to another child who will appreciate her.' She gave her to Mark's sister, Deborah.

"Deborah called me Pirette. She loved me for a little while and put me on her bed. Pretty soon she was too old to pay attention to dolls. She wanted to be with her friends. So I was back on the shelf again. I was very sad. I had dust in my hair, and my red velvet dress began to fade.

"One day Deborah's little sister Sandra grabbed me and took me to her room which, I must tell you, was an awful mess. She had the measles and was bored. She pulled out some of my hair and ripped the buttons off my dress. I cried myself to sleep. Needless to say, I refused to speak to Sandra, which made her very angry. She was putting red spots on my face when her mother took me away. She fixed my hair and my clothes and washed my face. She asked Mark if he thought Alison would like me and treat me well."

Denise paused. She took a deep breath. "I have finished. I hope you understood my English. It is an ordinary story, I am sure. For some children, dolls are not very special. Well, here I am with a family at last, and I am very happy here. I have good friends to be with. Also, I told Nettie yesterday that French dolls are very practical, no matter how elegant they may appear. We have to keep busy to be happy. What can I do here?"

"Would you like to be a nurse, too?" Alison asked.

"Yes, but I do not see the need for another nurse right now. Who is sick? Nettie and Boodles can take care of things."

Alison had an idea. "Can you sew, Denise?"

Denise's eyes lit up. "Can I sew? What a question to ask a French doll. That is the first thing we learn. I am not an expert like some dolls, but, to give you an answer, Mademoiselle Alison, yes, I can sew."

Chapter Twelve

Back in bed, Alison thought about what would become of the doll hospital. Nettie had come to her room to visit. She was busy chattering about the clothes she wanted Denise to make for her. Alison wasn't paying too much attention.

"What about the hospital, Nettie?" Alison finally asked. "We have a hospital and two nurses and a doctor and no patients."

"It can be a sewing room again," Nettie suggested. "I can learn to sew. Denise and I will make it our sewing room. We'll make you something nice."

"I don't need anything," Alison said. "All I wear is pajamas. I think the hospital should stay a hospital. Christopher gets a cold once in a while. You might get something, too, Nettie. Maybe if I am really sick again, I could move into our hospital, and all of you could take care of me. Mama could have a rest."

"You're too big, Alison. We couldn't lift you up or help you to the bathroom or carry your tray. We can only look after dolls or furries in the hospital. Anyway, clothes are just as interesting. Denise said she would start by making me an apron. Can you get some scraps of material from your mother? That's all we need right now. She left her sewing basket in the back of the closet."

Nettie climbed off the bed to go discuss a new wardrobe with Denise. Alison was not satisfied with what Nettie had said. After all, they *had* nursed Denise back to good health. That was pretty important, and it made Alison feel good. She supposed she wasn't any better than usual, but she felt different. She still had to spend most of the day in bed, and she still ached as the day wore on. But when she was busy with the hospital she wasn't thinking about herself, so it really did seem that she was better.

We'll have a meeting tonight, she decided. We'll meet in the hospital and close the door and talk about what we should do. Christopher will be able to tell us what is best, or at least make some suggestions. She wasn't sure they should rely on Christopher. He wasn't in the house all that much. She and Boodles and Nettie and Denise were the ones who had to decide.

"We're having a meeting at seven-thirty, Christopher," Alison told her brother when he came to take away the supper tray.

"Who's having a meeting?"

"All of us; a meeting in the hospital. We have to decide something."

Christopher looked at the clock. "What about my program? It's already started. How about tomorrow night at seven? Or tomorrow morning, even?"

Christopher had seen the TV space show at least 100 times, Alison was certain. He had been watching it since he was her age. He could miss one night. "Please, Christopher. We have a project. We need your help."

"Okay, I guess. I'll be right back."

What project? Alison wondered. She had to think up something quick or Christopher would be impatient to watch his television. It was hard to keep his attention very long unless he was really interested in what you were doing.

Christopher sat beside the door, next to Boodles. He scratched the dog's head. "We're outnumbered by the girls, Boodles, three to two. What do you think they have in store for us?"

Alison began to explain. "All of us, all of us

except Christopher, who has a paper route, should have something to do. It will make us feel better. Sewing is all right, but Boodles can't do it and I don't think I'd be very good at it. What will we use this room for?"

"It is a nice room," Denise said. "It would be a shame not to use it. When I first came here, I remember, I thought that it was the nicest room I could ever have to be sick in."

"You enjoyed being in charge of the hospital, didn't you, Nettie?" Alison asked.

"Yes, but I have to have something to be in charge of. I can't order Denise around, and Boodles never listens to what I tell him to do."

"I like it in here," Boodles said, "even if Nettie does get after me."

Christopher looked bored. "I can't think of anything for you to do in here, except sew."

Alison had an inspiration. "Listen to me. What do you say if we keep the hospital? All we need is patients, isn't that right?"

"You certainly can't have a hospital without patients," Christopher said. "Do you have any old dolls in your room upstairs? You could look after them."

Nettie spoke up. "Of course she doesn't, you know that, Christopher. I was Alison's first doll. She never needed another one."

"You're out of luck, Alison. No sick dolls, no hospital."

Now it was the moment to tell them her inspiration. "Other children have sick dolls and injured dolls, don't they, Christopher? We could look after them."

"You're right, Alison, but they are not going to walk over here for us to look after them. They don't even know we're here. I have to look at my program." He started to stand up.

"Wait a minute, Christopher. You could bring them here on your bicycle and take them back when they are well."

"Alison," Christopher answered patiently, "how will they know about the doll hospital? How will they know about me? Sure I can bring them and take them back, but first you have to find them. How?"

"Sit back down, Christopher, and I will tell you."

Chapter Thirteen

Alison explained what they could do. They would make up an announcement about their hospital. Mama could type it up, and Dad would take it to his office to make a lot of copies. Christopher would put a copy inside each newspaper he delivered. "We can figure out the rest of it later on. What do you think?"

Christopher was impressed. He sat back down. Alison could see that he was turning the idea over in his head. He bit his lower lip and nodded his head slightly.

"Twenty-seven houses on my paper route," he said half to himself. "There are bound to be kids in most of them. I see toys and stuff on the lawns or the front porches. We should distribute at least three announcements, like over a two-week stretch. That's almost a hundred copies. We can allow for a few extra, too. I will tack a couple to the utility poles. What do you say, Boodles? Is it a good idea?"

"As long as you take furries, too. It isn't only dolls who get sick. Don't you remember when I had trouble with my ear? Alison's mother had to sew it back on."

"Christopher and Boodles say yes," Alison said. "What about you, Denise?"

"Oh, yes, I would like to help. We will need beds, of course. I can make the sheets and pillows."

"And you, Nettie?"

"I suppose it's all right if it's what you want, Alison. I can learn to sew later. If we get too many patients, I want Boodles to understand he will have to be a night nurse, too."

"That's all right with me," Boodles said. "I can look after the furries."

"Fine," Alison said. "We all agree. Tomorrow morning we will meet after breakfast. We will decide what to put in the announcement and what we have to do to get ready."

Christopher came to the meeting the next morning with a piece of paper in his hand. "It's only a draft — that means something that can be changed, Nettie. You can add to it or take parts away or even say it's no good, and we'll start over. Let me read it to you."

Christopher cleared his throat. "Up at the top in big letters we'll have 'DOLL HOSPITAL OPENS.' I'll write that with Magic Markers. 'Experienced staff . . .' What is it, Nettie?"

"*Experienced*, please. I want to know what I am."

Christopher groaned. "*Experienced* means you know what you are doing because you have done it before."

Nettie smiled with satisfaction.

"Please, Nettie, no more questions until I have finished. Where was I? Oh, 'Experienced staff ready to take immediate care of illness and injuries. Rehabilitation program' — wait until I finish, Nettie — 'available.'

"Then, on a single line, in big letters, but not as big as the others, 'NO CHARGE.'

"Next line: 'Permanent adoption may be arranged.' Is that all right, Alison?"

Alison looked around the room. Boodles and Nettie and Denise nodded yes.

"I don't know what you will do if too many patients want to stay here forever," Christopher observed.

"That's our worry, Christopher," Nettie said. "You may go on reading."

"The rest of the announcement has to do with

me. I tell anyone who has a sick doll or furry to call me between four and four-thirty, just before I start my delivery, and make arrangements for the pick-up.

"I put the names of the staff at the bottom. Alison J. Taggert has a new title: Director. She's the one who is in charge of the whole works. Nettie Taggert is promoted to head nurse. Boodles Taggert is head of the rehabilitation program. You take the patients for a walk, Boodles, and see to it they get enough exercise. Denise Alexandra Taggert is housekeeper. I signed the announcement, Christopher Taggert, D.D. (Doll Doctor) and Resident."

"What is *rehabilitation*?" Nettie asked at once.

"I just told Boodles, Nettie. Why don't you pay attention? You were so busy admiring your new title, you didn't hear me. Rehabilitation means getting the patients back on their feet again so they can go home."

No one had any comments. Christopher went off with his draft to ask his mother to type it for him.

Denise, the practical French doll, cast her eyes carefully around the room. "We will have to make some changes, don't you agree, Nurse Nettie?"

"Head Nurse Nettie, please, Denise, or just call me Nettie, if you like. Yes, we will have to make changes. We certainly don't have enough beds."

Alison frowned. Denise had moved right in and taken over. "I suppose that's the director's job. I'll talk to Mama. There is some old furniture in the basement. Christopher will paint it for us. He loves to use spray paint. He has painted his bicycle at least six times."

She had to go back to bed. Enough excitement for one morning, she told herself. Being a director was a tough job.

Chapter Fourteen

"Did you type Christopher's announcement, Mama?" Alison asked when she heard her mother straightening up her room. She looked at the clock. She had slept for close to three hours, after the meeting.

"Indeed, I did. Here it is. Christopher said you should look at it in case there are some final changes."

Alison couldn't read everything on the announcement, but she recognized enough to see that Christopher and Mama had made it just the way Christopher had read it to them in the doll hospital.

"See, Mama," she pointed to her name. "I am

the director. When is Dad going to make the copies?"

"I wanted to talk to you about this, Alison. I am afraid we'll have to wait until you see Dr. Long and get his okay."

"Why?" Alison protested. She had a heavy feeling in her stomach, the feeling she always had when she knew something bad was going to happen. "Why, Mama? We just saw him and he didn't say anything. He says I can do anything I feel like doing. He says I'll be the first to know when to stop. That's what he said, Mama. You heard him. Was it because I walked out to the kitchen?"

A tear ran down Alison's cheek. She wiped it away with her pajama sleeve. Her mother sat on the edge of the bed. She put her arm around Alison to draw her close.

"It is only a precaution, darling. Dr. Long says normal routine is one thing. You and he understand that. Strenuous activity is something else. Directors are pretty important, and he's afraid you will be too busy to look after yourself the way you have up to now. Tomorrow we'll go see him. If he gives you the go-ahead, Dad will make a hundred copies, and Christopher will distribute them, and maybe you'll soon have a room full of patients. But we have to wait."

Alison felt some relief. Dr. Long hadn't found

anything serious since she came back from the hospital in April, just her weight and dizziness and being sort of tired. She told herself he wouldn't find anything wrong tomorrow. Something was usually going wrong, Alison knew. She was used to it by now. She would have to tell her friends to wait, that was all. In the meantime she could still begin to do her job.

"Do you have any more of those apple and pear boxes, Mama? They are the beds. Christopher can paint them and we'll fix them up with sheets and pillows."

"I was just thinking about those boxes, baby. I looked in the doll hospital. Nettie was asleep in one and Denise in the other, just where you put them. You must have forgotten Boodles and left him in the closet."

Alison figured it still wasn't the time to tell her mother about her friends. Someday, but not now. An appointment with Dr. Long was enough for today.

Her mother was still talking. "These fruit boxes made me remember when your father and I were first married. We had a little apartment close to the law school. We had no money and no furniture. We collected boxes from the fruit store and used them to put our books in. I remember the different labels we found. They were so lovely we didn't want to put paint over them.

71

We still have them, piled up in the basement. You may have as many as you want, but I'll wash them and cover them with old sheets or something. I don't want them painted. Does that sound silly?"

Alison shook her head. Denise could make covers for the boxes. Her parents' apartment sounded pretty interesting. "What did you sleep on?" she said. "What did you eat on?"

"We had a mattress on the floor for a while before we bought a bed. Someone threw out an ugly kitchen table and two even uglier chairs. We took them home. Those I did paint, you may be sure."

"How did you get money?" Alison wanted to know. Money didn't mean much to her, but it seemed important to everyone else.

"I had a job while Dad was in law school. It wasn't much of a job — just office work — but it kept us going. Then he went into the law firm here and I had Christopher and then I had you and here we are sitting together on your bed talking about old times when I should be fixing your lunch tray. Soup and sandwich for lunch sound all right?"

Chapter Fifteen

Dr. Long said something to Mama when he opened the door to his office. What it was Alison couldn't hear, but Mama said to her, "I think I'll wait outside today, darling. You are a big girl now. You don't need me tagging along after you every place."

That seemed odd. As far back as Alison could remember, her mother always went into the doctor's office with her. She noticed something else. The woman in the office was the same one who had been there the last time, the one who talked into the phone a lot.

And Nettie wasn't with her. She told Alison that since this wasn't a regular important visit, she preferred to stay home and help Denise get the hospital ready for patients. Alison wasn't sure Nettie was telling the truth, but she didn't object. Mostly, Nettie and Denise sat on their pillows under the window and talked. As soon as the hospital was ready for business, Alison intended to put a stop to that.

She was so busy thinking about her project, Alison didn't hear Dr. Long talking to her.

He was saying, "Your mother said you were starting a doll hospital. I thought I better have another look before you take on such a responsibility. Do you think you can handle it?"

"I don't know," Alison answered honestly. "I want to try." She went on to tell Dr. Long she wasn't sure she was really better, she just felt better when she was thinking about the hospital project.

Dr. Long agreed. "It's important to have an interest in something. Television can be pretty boring, can't it? Well, let's have a look."

Alison lifted herself up on the table without his help. "Leave your blouse on, Alison, this isn't a serious visit," Dr. Long said.

He listened to her heart. He looked into her ears and throat, finally, into her eyes. He pressed under her arms, then under her ears. Alison drew in her breath sharply.

"It still hurts a little, does it, Alison?"

"Yes, but maybe not so much. I can't be sure.

I always jump when you do that."

Dr. Long laughed. "I have noticed. You can get down now."

Alison eased herself off the table and walked over to the scale in the corner.

"You're trained now, aren't you, Alison?" Dr. Long joked. "Let's see what it says."

He fiddled with the scales. Alison watched his face. Dr. Long raised his eyebrows and fiddled some more. The little red numbers flickered.

"Okay," the doctor said. "You haven't lost half an ounce. You're just the same as the last time we weighed you. Your mother must be feeding you pretty well. Is that right?"

"I am a little hungrier than I used to be," Alison answered. "I ate a whole big hamburger the other day."

"That's important," Dr. Long said. "Sit down for a minute, Alison, and we'll have a talk. I want you to know that I think the doll hospital is a good idea. I am going to tell your mother that. By now you know when something is bothering you and you have to rest. Keep on with the naps, Alison. And don't push it. Let your dolls do the work. Where is my old friend, Nettie, today?"

"She stayed home to talk to Denise."

"Oh, Denise. A new friend or a patient?"

"Both." Alison explained who Denise was and

how she had had the measles. Dr. Long nodded. "It's a good thing you were there to look after her. Measles can be pretty tough." He took her to the door. He asked her mother to come in.

"We'll go straight home," Mama said when she came out. "You can call your father and tell him to run off a hundred copies of your announcement. I'll go by and pick them up this afternoon so Christopher can deliver them. I have scrubbed the apple boxes. I'll start covering them tomorrow."

"That's Denise's job, Mama. She's the housekeeper. All we need are the boxes and the old sheets. Oh, yes, and some nice old pillows if you have them."

"That's a big job, Alison. Are you certain Denise can handle it?" her mother asked. "You'll tell me if she can't, promise?"

"Yes, Mama."

"Christopher said you had to have a low table and a bureau and a little cabinet. We can take care of those things. Christopher said he would spray-paint them white."

Her mother stopped the car in front of the house. "It's nap time as soon as you call your father."

"Let me talk to Mama, Princess," Dad said after he had taken her order for the hundred copies. She gave the phone to her mother. "I can get to bed by myself."

Alison shut the hallway door. She leaned back against the wall to listen.

"She's holding her own, Ted. Dr. Long doesn't know quite what to make of it. He's going to talk to his friends in Boston. He said we should think about striking back before it's really necessary. He didn't say what he meant."

Alison couldn't make out the rest of what her mother said. 'Strike back,' what did that mean? It didn't sound like anything worth asking Christopher about. She would wait for bigger words than "strike back."

Chapter Sixteen

Christopher reported to the meeting that he had delivered the announcements. He didn't expect any phone calls right away, and he warned Alison and her friends they might not receive any at all. He had no idea how kids felt about sending their dolls and furries off to a strange hospital. "Don't get your hopes too high," he cautioned before he went off to look at his program.

Denise was sewing on the cover for the second apple box. At one end of the box was a label with the picture of an Indian with a feather in his hair. Denise said she planned to leave the label uncovered. She sewed very carefully, making tiny tight stitches and binding the corners where the sheet slipped over the box.

"Not so fast, Nettie," she advised the head nurse who was having trouble sewing a straight line. "Smaller stitches, or it will all pull out. Let me finish that one, Nettie. You can't learn to sew in one day."

"I'm a nurse, not a seamstress," Nettie grumped. "I just wanted to learn in case I had to sew Boodles' ear back on or something like that."

"That's the doctor's job, Nettie," Alison said. "Your job is to take care of the patients, not operate on them."

"But I plan to be a doctor someday," Nettie protested. "First, I'll be the head nurse, then when Christopher goes off, I'll be the doctor. I have to start practicing now."

"We'll see about that when the time comes," Alison said. "We don't even have any patients yet. Christopher may be right. Kids might be afraid to send their dolls to us. I wouldn't want to go off to a strange hospital and strange doctors. We'll have to wait and see. You should learn to sew while you are waiting, Nettie. You may not have a chance later on."

Denise looked up from her work. "We'll have those beds ready by tomorrow evening. Christopher told us before you came in, Alison, that the table will be here at noon. He painted it last night and again this morning."

Alison listened all the next morning for the phone to ring. She had left the hospital door open so she would not miss it. The phone did not ring. No one was supposed to call until four o'clock, but you could never tell. She washed the baseboards of the room with a damp cloth. One side a day, mother had said, giving her the cleaner. By afternoon nap time the baseboard under the window was sparkling white. She reached up and cleaned the windowsill as well. She felt good as she stretched out on her bed, and was soon fast asleep.

She did not hear the phone ring long before four o'clock and Christopher's excited voice as he talked. Only after he repeated himself, did Alison hear him say, "Alison, wake up. I'm going off to pick up our first patient. It's over on Hilltop Drive. I think it's an emergency. All of you be ready when I get back."

Alison sat up. She was still fuzzy from her noontime pill and her long nap. She hadn't heard everything Christopher had said. "What? You have a doll for us?"

"I think so," Christopher said. "I only have a minute. This kid called. Mama said he was crying. He wanted to talk to me. The kid — it was a boy — said Looey was falling apart and could I come quick and save him. His mother came to the phone to tell me where they lived. She said they were all very fond of Looey, but he was getting old and they would understand if we couldn't help him. I told her we would try. Mama gave me a canvas bag to carry him in. Okay, I'm off. You have the staff ready."

Head Nurse Nettie adjusted the white cap Denise had made for her. "Our first case, except for Denise," she told Boodles. "He will probably need a lot of rehabilitation. Have you practiced everything I taught you?"

"Over and over again," Boodles said. "You don't need much practice to walk from the window to the door and back again."

"You never know," Nettie replied. "The patient may lose a leg. Then you will see how difficult it is."

"Oh, Nettie," Denise said. "Don't say these dreadful things. Christopher will be able to make him well. Looey, that sounds like a French name. Do you suppose he is French like me?"

Alison tacked a white towel over the table. "Lay out the operating stuff, Nettie."

Nettie put a pair of scissors, cotton swabs, and a roll of bandages on the table.

"Boodles and I will stay out of the way and watch," Denise said.

Alison was so excited she couldn't sit still. Heart pounding, she paced back and forth until she heard the clang of Christopher's bicycle as he let it fall against the front porch. His steps sounded down the hall. Before he reached the hospital door, he shouted, "Get ready. It's a real emergency. We have to pull him through."

Chapter Seventeen

Christopher put a canvas bag on the hospital table. Carefully he took something from the bag and stretched it out on the table. Nettie gasped. Denise turned her head away. Boodles swallowed twice. Alison could not believe her eyes.

What was left of a doll lay on the table before them. One arm was attached by only a thread. Stuffing was poking out of its stomach. The doll had only one leg. Where the other leg had been was an empty hole. The doll's head was cracked in three places.

Christopher looked inside the bag. "Here it is," he said. He put the missing leg on the table next to the doll.

"What happened?" Alison whispered.

"I'm not sure," Christopher answered. "The kid said he had an accident; he was crying so hard I had trouble understanding him. He kept howling, 'Looey, Looey,' so I guess the poor little thing must be a boy. He's such a mess, it's hard to tell."

"Ohhh," Denise cried. "Will he be all right? It is worse than the measles."

"Let's get started." Christopher ordered. "Alison, would you bring in a soft, wet washcloth. Denise, prepare a needle with strong thread. Head Nurse Nettie, there's a tube of glue on Dad's desk. Please get it. We'll do Looey's head first."

Nettie and Alison scurried into the next room. In the bathroom Alison pressed warm water through the washcloth. She rubbed it over the bar of soap. Plain water wasn't going to take the grease and dirt from Looey's face and bald head. She wet half a hand towel to wipe the soap off. She would use the other half to dry him.

Christopher examined the cracks in Looey's head. "They are awfully big," he told Alison. "Clean them out as well as you can. While you do that I have to find some adhesive tape."

Alison washed Looey's face. Beneath the grime she discovered his eyes were blue. At least they used to be blue. There was a touch of red left on his lips. Next she scrubbed the doll's head. There was one crack across his forehead, one in the middle, and an enormous crack across the back of his head.

Looey's hair had been painted on when he was new. It was brown, Alison guessed, and curly. She wiped carefully around the cracks until most of his head was clean. Then she looked closely at the cracks. They were filled with dirt. Alison wasn't brave enough to try to clean the dirt out. Where was Christopher? She looked around. He hadn't come back.

"I'll do that, Alison," Nettie said. Alison stepped aside. Nettie stood on an apple box. She took a Q-tip and ever so gently began to clean out the cracks.

"Does it hurt him?" Alison asked in a low voice.

"I don't think so," Nettie said. "He hasn't made a sound, and I have almost finished. He must be unconscious."

"Good work, Nettie," Christopher complimented the head nurse. "That's a perfect job. Give me the glue, please, and a swab."

Nettie handed Christopher the glue. He squeezed a bit on the swab. He rubbed the glue into the break. He squeezed Looey's head until the crack was closed. "Wipe off the glue, Nettie," he asked, "while I hold his head shut. Then find your cardboard and fan him. It won't take long. This is instant glue."

When Christopher had finished, he put a piece of tape over each crack. "That should hold him. He is beginning to look like a doll again. Are you ready, Denise?"

Denise climbed up in the apple box on the other side of the table. She had a needle with white nylon thread ready. "The leg first?" she asked Christopher.

"Yes. I'll hold it. You tell me what to do."

Denise studied the hole in Looey's body. She pushed up his leg and fitted it into the hole. "This is a very difficult task," she explained. "I don't have much to sew it to. I am afraid poor Looey will be short in one leg. Boodles will have a big job to rehabilitate him."

She sewed the leg tightly to the body. She tested what she had done. "I will go around one more time to make sure," she told Christopher. "The rest of the work will not be so hard. Tomorrow I will make him a hospital gown to get well in."

When Denise had finished, Looey looked like a doll again, a banged-up doll, yes, but a doll you could recognize, Alison thought. She picked him up from the table to carry him to the box Nettie had made ready under the window. Nettie pulled a sheet up to his chin and spread a cloth over the top of the box to keep the light out. "Shh," she said to everyone. "The patient has to sleep."

"Will he live?" Alison asked Christopher.

"It's hard to tell," he said. "Looey looks as though he had a pretty hard life even before the accident. The kid was sure worried about him, like he had lost a parent or someone. I'll give him a report on Looey's condition. He said he'd wait ouside his house until I delivered the paper."

He looked at his watch. "I'm late for my delivery. Looey is in your hands now, Alison. Take good care of him."

Chapter Eighteen

In the middle of the night Alison awoke. The room was dark. Her mother had come in, as she did every night when Alison was asleep, to pull down the shade and turn on the bathroom light. Alison could see only the glimmer of light under the door. She felt strange, almost out of place in her room, which wasn't her own room. It was how she felt when she was awakened in the hospital to take a pill. She didn't belong where she was, but she wasn't sure where she did belong. It was confusing.

She put her hands in back of her head. Staring up at the ceiling, she thought about what was going on. Something had awakened her from a deep sleep. It had not been a bad dream, she was certain. She heard the sound again, a slight rustling somewhere. It was probably the leaves in the breeze. She turned on her side and shut her eyes. She couldn't sleep. There were voices now that went with the rustling. Alison knew all the late-at-night noises. It wasn't her parents talking upstairs. It wasn't Christopher's radio which he sometimes left on when he fell asleep.

She listened with both ears. The sounds were close. They seemed to be coming from just the other side of the wall. They were from the hospital! Alison slipped out of bed. She tiptoed to the hospital door. She saw the edge of light underneath. She opened the door quietly. Across the room Nettie, Boodles, and Denise were gathered around Looey's bed. Alison crept across the room. "What's the matter?" she whispered.

Nettie took Alison's hand and drew her back across the room. "It's Looey," she said. "Something is wrong. Maybe we should call Christopher. He keeps kicking his sheet off and rolling his head from side to side. Every once in a while he makes a crazy noise. Do you think some of the glue dripped into his head? It had an awful smell."

Denise said something to Boodles in French. They talked back and forth for a minute.

"Denise says he may be delirious," Boodles told them.

"What's *delirious*?" Nettie asked.

Alison knew what it meant. "It's sort of when you have nightmares, Nettie, but you're not asleep. Sometimes it's a fever, sometimes it's the medicine they give you."

"Oh," said Nettie. "That sounds pretty bad. Looey doesn't have a fever, at least not a big one. I checked. We gave him half an aspirin. Would that make him delirious?"

"No," Alison responded. "He might be in shock from the operation. When something strange or bad happens to you, your body can't take it. Something like that is shock, I think."

Alison was wide awake by now. She wasn't dizzy at all. "Let's not wake Christopher up just yet. I'll hold Looey for a while. We'll see what happens. The rest of you go back to sleep. I'll call you if I need your help."

Boodles yawned. "That's a good idea. I'm sleepy."

"You promise to wake us?" Nettie asked.

"I promise. I'll go back to bed at seven before Mama wakes up."

Alison picked up the injured Looey. She wrapped a flannel baby blanket around him. She leaned back against the wall under the window. She could feel Looey jerk and twitch. He made noises Alison couldn't understand. She was tempted to carry him up to Christopher's room for a consultation, but Dr. Long had been quite firm against stairs. "If you fall, Alison," he had said, "it will make matters worse." She hummed to Looey and rocked him in her arms.

The patient slowly became calm. He lay still and silent. Alison put her head down. Yes, he was breathing. Whatever was wrong with Looey had gone away for a while. He was sleeping peacefully. He seemed comforted to have some-one holding him. Alison laid Looey in her lap. She put her head against the wall and closed her eyes.

At dawn she awoke, stiff from the uncom-fortable position. She put Looey in his bed. She crawled over to Nettie's bed. The Head Nurse was snoring. Oh, Nettie, Alison thought, what would I do without you? "I'm going back to bed now," she whispered. "Looey is all right. He's sleeping. Don't wake him up. Go on sleeping yourself."

Nettie grunted and rolled over on her stom-ach. Alison bent over and kissed her on the cheek. "You're a good head nurse, Nettie."

Alison curled up in her own bed. She heard her mother come down to the kitchen. Chris-topher thumped around overhead, looking for something to put on.

Mama came in and opened the shade and turned off the bathroom light. "Wake up, little

Alison. Christopher will have your breakfast tray here in a minute. Do you want help to get to the bathroom?"

Alison shook her head. She rubbed her eyes and stretched, pretending to be waking up. "Oh," she said, "I had the strangest dream."

"Was it something scary, Alison?"

"No, it was a good dream. I wish it hadn't gone away." Later she would make something up about what happened last night in the hospital, something pretty close to the truth. She wanted her mother to know what went on there, even if she told her it was a dream.

"The same for breakfast?" Mama asked.

"I think I can eat two eggs this morning. I'm real hungry for some reason."

Her mother smiled. "Maybe the dream gave you an appetite. Two eggs it is."

Chapter Nineteen

Christopher had scarcely taken away Alison's breakfast tray when Boodles scooted into the bedroom. He stood on his hind legs to scratch at Alison's sheet. "Alison," he panted, "Head Nurse Nettie wants you to come quick. We are having terrible troubles with Looey."

Alison hopped out of bed and followed Boodles into the hospital. Nettie on one side and Denise on the other were holding the patient down in his apple box bed. Looey was making all sorts of noises. Among them Alison heard him shout, "I want to go home, I want to go home."

"Goodness, what's the matter with Looey?"

Alison asked. "He was sound asleep when I left him."

"We were all asleep," Nettie explained in disgust. "We sat up all night, most of it anyway, until you came in, with this crazy doll after his operation. Be quiet, Looey, or we'll tie you down."

"That's no way to speak to a patient in a hospital, Nettie," Alison told her. "Let me talk to him."

Looey opened his eyes and looked up. He saw Alison leaning over his bed. He stopped kicking and shouting.

"What is it, Looey?" Alison asked. "Do you hurt somewhere?"

Looey shook his bandaged head. "Home," he muttered. "I want to go home."

"You are not well. You had a serious operation yesterday. You must rest. Then you will have rehabilitation. After that, we will talk about going home."

"It's out of the question," Head Nurse Nettie snapped. "You have to stay here and let us nurse you. Those are the rules."

"Please, Nettie," Alison said, "let me talk to him." She picked up the doll and held him on her lap. "You don't even have any clothes. Tell me why it's so important to go home right away."

"Roy needs me. He won't sleep without me. He won't eat without me. He won't go to play-school without me. He won't do anything without me."

"Who is this Roy?" Nettie interrupted. "What kind of a silly kid is he? He certainly didn't look after you very well. You were a wreck when Christopher brought you to the hospital."

"Nettie, please," Alison said again. "Who is Roy, Looey?"

"He's the little kid where I live. I sort of look after him. He won't do anything unless I tell him to do it. He won't mind his mother or father or even his brothers. I brought them all up, I did. I've been the family doll for a long time."

Alison was very curious. "What do you mean, 'the family doll'? Nettie's right, Looey. You are in awful shape. You look like a junkyard doll."

"That's because Roy rode over me on his new bike. He couldn't help it. I was on the handlebars and fell off. He rode over me and dragged me into a mud puddle. That's all I can remember, going into the mud puddle. But I'm all right now. I'm used to being knocked around." Looey looked up at Alison. "What's your name?"

"Alison. I am the director of the hospital. This is Head Nurse Nettie, and the doll with the long hair is Denise. And Boodles, he's the dog over by the door. Christopher is the doctor. He brought you here and fixed you up."

"Ask him to take me home, please. They will be worried about me."

"Roy was worried about you, all right. He called up and asked for our ambulance. He was crying hard, Christopher said."

"He cries a lot. He's still a baby in lots of ways. His brothers don't cry, nosiree."

"How many brothers are there?"

"Four: Tom, the oldest; Pete; Al; and Larry. I brought them all up. Tom is almost sixteen now. It's been a big job. I'll come back and see you after I bring Roy up. Now, I have to go."

"We can't hold him here against his will, Nettie," Alison said. "He looks healthy enough to take care of himself. I'll see how his head is. Alison peeled back a piece of tape. Christopher had done a good job. The cracks were sealed together tight.

Next she moved his legs. "How do they feel, Looey?"

"Great," Looey said. He climbed off her lap. "Watch!" He ran over to Boodles and ran back.

"Let's see you do it twenty times, Looey," Nettie said sarcastically. "And stand on your sore head for five minutes. Have you noticed you haven't any clothes on?"

"Nettie, stop it. We'll let him go home after

he is dressed. Denise, can you make him some overalls this morning?"

"I can do that, also some pants and a shirt to take with him."

"Good. Now listen to me, Looey. Back to bed and rest while Denise makes you some clothes. Christopher will take you to Roy this afternoon on his paper delivery. That's the best we can do for you."

"Okay, I guess," said Looey. "I'll come back if something else awful happens to me. This isn't such a bad place except for her." Looey pointed to Nettie. "I don't get along with girl dolls."

"You mustn't feel that way, Looey. Nettie saved your life. If it weren't for her, you wouldn't be going home to your friend Roy this afternoon."

Looey put his head down. Without looking at Nettie, he muttered, "I'm sorry, Head Nurse, I didn't mean that."

"That's all right," Nettie sniffed. "I don't pay attention to what delirious patients say."

Chapter Twenty

Looey fussed and fought as Denise and Alison dressed him in the blue corduroy coveralls Denise had made out of a pair of Christopher's old pants. "Look at the red buttons, Looey," Alison said. "They go all the way down the front."

"You look quite smart, Looey, if I do say so myself," Denise told him.

"You were a mess when you came into the hospital yesterday," Nettie reminded Looey. "Now you are going home clean and well-dressed. You ought to be grateful to us."

"All I want is jeans and a T-shirt," Looey said. "This is sissy stuff. Roy will tease me. So will the others."

"Roy will not tease you, Looey," Alison assured him. "Christopher called him on the telephone this morning. He was still crying about what happened to you on his bicycle. He promised Christopher he will look after you better from now on."

"Here you are, Looey," Denise said. She handed him a neatly folded pair of jeans and two T-shirts. "We will put them in the bag with you. Change into them when you are home, if you must. Just remember that this is a French coverall you have on. It is very fashionable. Also, it will keep you from getting dirty again."

Looey was still grumbling under his breath when there was a tap at the door. Alison's mother looked in. "Is the patient ready to go? Christopher is packing his papers. He asked me to bring Looey out. He said to tell you he had a phone call. It sounds as though you will have another patient this evening."

She bent down and picked up Looey. "You're Looey, are you? I didn't see you last night. Christopher said you had a bad accident and he was going to have to operate. You certainly look healthy this morning. What a lovely jumpsuit. Wherever did you get that? Christopher had some pants the very same color."

Looey did not answer. Denise stole a look at

Alison, who pretended to be busy making Looey's bed. Nettie kept as quiet as a mouse. Boodles shut his eyes.

Alison finished the bed. She took the canvas bag to her mother. She asked her mother to put Looey inside very carefully. "Tell Christopher to take it easy with him. He is probably still a little sore after all he has been through. Who do you suppose the next patient will be?"

"I don't know. Perhaps this one will stay longer. I think I heard Christopher say something about being lost. You will find out soon enough. You haven't had your nap yet, have you, Alison?"

Alison hadn't. They were all so busy getting Looey ready to go home, she had forgotten — not really forgotten, she supposed, just postponed — her nap. She hadn't felt tired the way she generally felt after lunch.

"I am going to take it now, Mama. Tell Christopher to wake me when he comes back. They may need me in the hospital with the new patient."

Alison went to her room and kicked off her slippers. She lay back to sleep, but her head was filled with excitement and expectations. The doll hospital was a success. They had cured Denise, and in only one day they had cured a major accident victim and sent him home. She won-

dered who the next patient would be. She sort
of hoped it would be a girl doll, although in a
hospital you couldn't really choose who your
patients were. Boys were a mess, she knew this
from school. They talked when they shouldn't
and pushed each other around. If it hadn't been
for Nettie they would have had trouble with
Looey, she thought. Nettie wasn't afraid of anybody. Alison giggled, remembering how Nettie
had shouted at Looey. She never would have
been able to do that, even though she was the
director of the hospital.

Christopher's bike clanged against the brick
steps. Alison looked up at the clock. He had been
gone only an hour. That was pretty fast. Usually
he didn't make it back until a quarter to six.
Maybe there was another emergency. She had
better be ready. She put her feet in her slippers
and went into the bathroom to wash her hands
against germs. She saw herself in the mirror.
She looked a tiny little bit fatter in the face, she
thought, and her eyes were brighter. The treatment was working at last. Now she would have
more time to spend in the doll hospital. There
were lots of things that needed to be done. She
couldn't put them all off on the staff.

Christopher and Alison arrived at the hospital
door at the same time. "Who is it, Christopher?"
she asked.

"I don't know," he replied. "He is an orphan, I guess, although he's pretty old to be an orphan." He put the hospital delivery bag on the table and pulled out a dirty old gray rabbit.

"That's not a doll," Nettie said immediately. "This is a doll hospital."

"We wrote 'furries' in the announcement, Nettie," Christopher said. "This is a furry, at least I think it is. What do you say, Boodles?"

"It *was* a furry," Boodles replied after taking a close look at the rabbit. "I guess it still is. Where did you find him?"

"I didn't. Miss Potter did. She found him on the street at the end of her driveway. She thinks he must have fallen out of a car. She took him in and dried him off. Then she took him up and down the street, but no one claimed him. She had read our announcement, so she called us up."

Alison took charge. "First of all, he has to have a bath. I'll wash him in my tub with shampoo. Can you use Mama's hair dryer, Christopher? You come help me, Boodles. This is your patient. You can dry him off first in my towel. Then we'll see what needs to be done."

Chapter Twenty-One

The gray rabbit trembled when Alison put him in the tub and squeezed warm water over him.

"Rabbits don't like water the way we dogs do, Alison," Boodles said. "They wash themselves with their tongues and wash their faces with their front paws."

"I'll hurry up," Alison said. "Hand me the shampoo." She rubbed the baby shampoo into the poor old rabbit's fur. He trembled even more and sneezed. The bathtub water turned black. Alison rinsed him with the hand shower as well as she could. He sniffled as she turned him over to Boodles to dry. "He certainly smells better," she said. "I don't believe he's ever had a bath. Give him a good rub. Christopher will finish

drying him with the hair dryer."

Nettie and Denise held the wriggling rabbit while Christopher blew him dry. He was very frightened. His eyes rolled with terror. When Christopher finished, Denise used a soft baby hair brush she had found in the sewing basket to brush the rabbit's fur until it was sleek and silky. The rabbit shook himself and straightened his shoulders.

"I can't get his ears to stand up," Denise said. "He looks in good shape now except for his ears."

The gray rabbit spoke. "They are not supposed

to stand up. I am a lop-eared rabbit. My ears stay down," he said in a voice that sounded old and tired.

"Oh," said Denise. "So you are a loppy. You must be a French rabbit. I have never seen one, but I have heard tell of French loppies."

"Perhaps I am French. I do not know. I am so old I have almost forgotten where I came from."

Christopher was very interested in the rabbit he had brought home. "How do you know you are so old? You look like a regular rabbit to me, except for your ears. What do you say, Boodles?"

"You are right. He is no older than I am, and I am not as old as Nettie. How old are you, Nettie?"

"That's none of your business, Boodles. Only Alison knows, and she's not telling, are you, Alison? Do you have a name, rabbit? And do you have something wrong with you? This is a hospital, not a beauty parlor."

"Nettie," Alison scolded. "You must not talk that way or we will never have any patients. You shouted at Looey and made him angry. Now you are insulting our first furry."

"I have a name, all right," said the rabbit, "but I don't want to use it anymore." He stared down at his fur mournfully. "Look at me, I'm all gray.

I used to be a brown loppy with a white chest. Now I am gray all over." He sighed. "Why don't you call me Grandpa."

"That's great," Boodles piped up. "I never had a grandfather. I'll fix up a box for you and put it in the closet with mine. We furries have to stick together."

"My name is Alison. I am in charge of the hospital," Alison said.

"I am the doctor. Call me Christopher, Grandpa Rabbit."

"I am Denise, the housekeeper."

"I am the head nurse, Miss Nettie Taggert. All the patients have to do what I say. Are you a patient or a visitor?"

Grandpa Rabbit kicked his rear legs. He lifted his front legs over his ears. He shook his head from side to side. He blew his nose and gurgled deep in his throat. "Well, I don't know exactly. I don't feel sick. I don't think I have anything broken. I can see and hear and smell all right. I guess I am not a patient. I am just old. Do you have a place for old rabbits in your hospital? I don't have any place to go since I fell out of the car."

"Of course, we have a place for you, Grandpa Rabbit," Alison said. "Head Nurse Nettie has a good heart. She isn't used to being a head nurse yet. We all have jobs in the hospital. What would you like to do?"

"What do I know how to do?" the rabbit asked himself. He stroked his whiskers back with his paws. "I can tell stories," he finally said. "I must remember a thousand stories or more by now. I can even tell you all about myself now, if you have time. That way you'll know who, or what, I am."

"If Christopher has time, that would be very nice," Alison said.

"It's fine with me," Christopher said.

"I will make it short," Grandpa Rabbit said. "I have had a long day, and my bed looks very inviting. Let me see. Yes, once upon a time there was a young loppy rabbit. He was the only loppy on the shelf. A young girl named Pip saw the loppy and told her mother she had to have him. No silly dolls for Pip. All she wanted was the brown loppy."

"Really," Nettie interrupted. "This is too much. Denise and I certainly are not silly dolls. I could say a word or two about dumb rabbits if I wanted to."

"Shh, Nettie," Denise said. "It is impolite to interrupt grandfathers. You may scold him later, if you wish."

"Thank you, Denise. Head Nurse Nettie and

I will end up good friends, I am certain. Where was I? Oh, yes. On Christmas Day, there I was under the tree, wrapped in Santa Claus paper. It was uncomfortable, I can tell you. What is it, Head Nurse Nettie?"

"Is this going to be a long story or the short story you promised? It is bedtime for the patients."

"But I am not a patient. I am a visitor. In fact, I don't see any patients here at the moment. Let me finish the story you all asked for. I will make it short. Tomorrow I will tell you a long story about a trip I once made to a strange place. Pip was delighted with her rabbit. She carried him off to her room and tied a ribbon around his neck. She gave him a special name. They loved each other for many years and told each other all their secrets.

"The loppy rabbit grew old. Pip went away. He waited patiently on her bed for her to return. She came back one day with a little girl. It was hers. She gave the rabbit to the little girl. "This was my bestest friend," Pip said. "Now he is yours to love and look after."

"Not for long, alas," Grandpa Rabbit said. "The little girl put me alongside her on the seat of a car. When she got out on a strange street, the old rabbit fell to the ground. Then he was rescued by a young prince and taken to a castle where there were three young princesses to look after him and listen to his stories. End of story. Come along, Boodles. Show me to my room. Good-night, all."

Head Nurse Nettie wiped a tear from her eye with the hem of her apron. "Did anybody ever hear such foolishness?" she grumped.

Chapter Twenty-Two

When the lights were out all over the house, Nettie snuggled into Alison's bed. "Are you awake, Alison?" she asked softly.

"Yes. I was lying here thinking what a good hospital we had."

"Maybe. But we are going to have trouble with that old rabbit," Nettie complained. "I wish we had never let Boodles invite furries here. It's a doll hospital. That's what it says on the door."

"Boodles is a furry," Alison reminded Nettie. "He's your best friend."

"That's because he was the only friend I had. Now I have Denise."

Alison laughed. "Nettie, all you really like to do is fuss. When Denise first came to see us, you were jealous. You even had Boodles making faces at her. Now you say she's your best friend. Tomorrow Grandpa Rabbit will be your best friend, too. You both like to talk a lot. I think he is sort of bossy like you. You have a lot in common. Don't be a silly doll, Nettie. Head nurses have to be serious when they are on the job. Why don't you spend the night here? You won't have to listen to Boodles snore. Tomorrow night you may have some patients to attend to."

Alison was right. The next afternoon Nettie did have patients to look after; two, to be exact, named Amy and Becky. They were twins. And they were babies. And they cried all through the night.

"Kristen Moffat — do you remember her, Alison? She said you were in her class last year — gave them to me," Christopher explained.

"That's awful," Denise objected. "You can't give your baby dolls away. In France they would forbid that."

"She had to," Christopher said. "She got the twins for her birthday, and they haven't stopped yelling for a minute, she said. The other dolls couldn't sleep. She says she will take them back when they are grown up a little bit. You have to admit, they are kind of cute."

Christopher picked one of the dolls up. The baby's eyes opened. They were bright blue. She smiled and settled down in Christopher's arms.

"Which one is that?" Nettie asked.

Christopher looked at the foot of the doll's sleepsuit. A red *A* was stitched on the bottom. "This is Amy. Kristen said their clothes were all marked with an A or a B."

"Then this must be Becky," Nettie said. She took Becky from the table to hold her. Becky began to scream. Nettie put her down. She scowled. "Yesterday, a rabbit. Today, twins. What will be next, do you suppose, Alison?"

"Maybe she wants her bottle," Alison said. The bottle was tied around the doll's neck. Alison put the nipple in the doll's mouth. Becky smiled and started to suck.

"They will both fit in the same box for a while," Denise said. "Tomorrow I will make some baby sheets, blue and pink. Then I will make some baby clothes as soon as I finish Grandpa Rabbit's jacket."

"I will take them for a walk," Boodles said. "Get me a shoebox, Christopher, and some string. I can pull them around to keep them quiet."

"And you will tell them stories, won't you, Grandpa Rabbit?" Alison asked. "Amy and Becky will be much better looked after in the doll hospital than they were at Kristen's, don't you think, Head Nurse Nettie?"

"Maybe," Nettie said. "They are kind of cute, but if they howl all night I don't know what I am going to do."

The twins did howl most of the night. Alison could hear them as she turned over in bed. She felt sorry for Nettie, but, she told herself, Nettie was the head nurse. Besides, she had lots of help. Alison had to look after herself or Dr. Long would make her stay out of the doll hospital.

Early in the morning, Alison tiptoed next door. There was not a sound inside. Nettie and Denise were asleep in their beds. Boodles was stretched out snoring on the floor under the window. The closet door was closed almost tight. Alison

peeped in. Grandpa Rabbit was leaning back in the corner. Asleep in his lap side by side were Amy and Becky.

Alison felt warm and happy. She remembered that when she was first very sick Mama and Dad had sat by her bed upstairs, nursing her through the night. Each time she awoke, Dad or Mama would take her hand and give it a little squeeze. Now her dolls and furries were looking after the patients the same way. That was good.

I know what I'll do, she thought. I'll have my breakfast in the kitchen. She heard her mother and father moving around upstairs; not a sound yet from Christopher. Some mornings he liked to sleep late. I'll surprise them, she thought. She washed her face with cold water. She saw in the mirror that her hair was tangled up. She had been too busy to brush it after the twins showed up. She brushed it now and put in the silver barette Aunt Lil had brought her from Mexico. She put on her slippers and bathrobe and walked steadily out to the kitchen. She wasn't the least bit dizzy.

Mama wasn't there yet. Alison put three glasses on the counter. She filled them with orange juice and put them at the places on the table. She folded three napkins. A spoon for Dad who only drank his juice and a cup of coffee. A spoon and a knife and a plate for Mama who ate two pieces of brown bread toasted. Ugh. Alison hated that brown bread.

And for herself, a bowl of sugar cereal. She hadn't had sugar cereal in a long time. When she wasn't feeling well, it tasted sicky. She filled the bowl with Christopher's honey oats. She chewed one dry. It was really good.

"Alison, what are you up to?" her mother asked. "Why, you have set the table. What a sweetheart you are." She hugged Alison tightly against her. "Look, Ted," she said to Dad. "Look who we have for breakfast."

Chapter Twenty-Three

After the twins came to the doll hospital, there were no more patients for Christopher to pick up. It was just as well, Alison decided, because Amy and Becky needed a lot of attention. As a matter of fact, everyone in the hospital said that they were *not* the best babies in the world. But they were the cutest. Even Nettie agreed to that.

"It certainly hasn't been the same," she confided to Alison. "In some ways it has been more fun. We don't have time to listen to Grandpa Rabbit's dumb stories. That's the twins' job now," Nettie laughed.

At the weekly meeting of the hospital staff, everyone agreed they shouldn't send out the second or third announcement for more patients until they had Amy and Becky under control. It wouldn't be fair to the new patients to have to listen to the twins yell. They would wait until the babies were sleeping through the night.

Alison explained all of this to her mother at the lunch table. Summer was over. Christopher had gone back to school. He was in the first year of high school, and it was pretty tough, he told his mother. He kept his paper route and he came to the weekly meetings at the doll hospital, but he didn't have much time for anything else. Alison now had to run the hospital without his help. She and Denise washed the twins and played with them while Grandpa Rabbit took his nap.

Alison felt she had to look after her mother, too. Without Christopher in the house, Mama was lonely, so Alison stayed in the kitchen after breakfast when Dad and Christopher had left. She ate lunch in the kitchen, too, and dried the dishes before she went to her room for her afternoon nap. She could see that Mama liked to have her around. She didn't look quite so worried, and she told Alison stories about her own childhood.

Sometimes, Alison came out to eat supper with the family, but not often. By the end of the day she was really tired, even though she felt better than she had in a long time. She remembered that she usually felt all right after a treatment at the hospital, but it wasn't quite like this. Before, she felt on the edge of getting worse again, a "relapse," her parents called it. Mama always seemed to be waiting for her relapse. It made Alison worry, too.

Now Mama didn't ask every day how she felt, she was so happy to have Alison with her. "I'm glad you didn't try to go back to school," she told Alison one day. "It's selfish, I suppose, but I really enjoy having you home and out of bed. If you miss a year or two, that's all right. You have a long life ahead of you to make them up." Then her mother's eyes started to water, and she reached for a Kleenex. She put her hand across the table to take Alison's hand. She held on to it for the longest time, squeezing, then letting go. Alison saw that her mother was worrying again. She had better talk about her hospital.

"Amy and Becky are growing up fast," she said. "They can crawl around now. Only one of them can fit in Boodles's wagon at a time. Each one has her own bed. Denise has sewn monograms on their sheets. They still like to cry in the middle of the night. I don't understand it."

"Just like you, darling," Mama said. "Christopher slept through after he was a month old. My baby Alison woke up right on schedule every night at two o'clock for her bottle. I told myself you just wanted to be held. It's a good thing you didn't have Nettie then. She probably would have walked out."

"Nettie would never walk out. She likes to fuss all the time so we will pay attention to her. That's Nettie's way. When the twins are too much for her, she sleeps with me and lets Grandpa Rabbit sit up with them. Do you suppose Kristen Moffat will want them back someday? We have gone to all the trouble of bringing them up."

"I don't think so," her mother said. "It looks to me as though she put them out for adoption."

"*Adoption*, what does that really mean?" Alison asked. "I know it's on our announcement, but I wasn't sure what it meant. Isn't it sort of a long stay or something?"

"*Adoption* is when the parents or a mother or a father can't look after a baby for some reason. They let someone else look after the child, another family or an orphanage. Sometimes the parents are sick or don't want the baby or have to work and can't look after it, or are awfully poor and don't want their baby to grow up poor. They feel the baby is better off with someone else who will love it and look after it. Probably Kristen has so many other dolls, she couldn't handle Amy and Becky."

That was a really good word, 'adoption.' Nettie had been pestering Alison about what it meant. Now she could give Nettie a good, long answer. Alison knew she would never put any of her dolls or furries out for adoption. The very thought of it made her sniffle.

She finished her peanut butter and jelly sandwich. "I better go back to bed," she said. "Today is when I have a checkup."

"Four o'clock. Afterward, I have a little shopping. Can Nettie spare you for a couple of hours?"

Alison nodded and headed back to her room. She felt a little dizzy, but not so much you'd notice it if you were doing something else. She recalled that late yesterday afternoon when she was rolling on the floor with the twins, her head had begun to spin. That was a bad sign. She huddled in bed and shut her eyes. She said a little prayer to herself that she had learned at Sunday School a long time ago. "Dear God," she whispered. "Please look after me until I can look after myself. Thank you. My name is Alison Jennifer Taggert."

Chapter Twenty-Four

Alison woke up from her nap scared. It seemed that she was scared even before she woke up. She had had a really bad dream. Afternoon dreams, for some reason, were worse than night dreams. She was back in the hospital. A nurse who looked a lot like Nettie was giving her a shot. Dr. Long was there, she was pretty sure, but the nurse kept calling him Dr. Boodles. Denise and the twins were laughing at some secret they shared. They rolled over at the bottom of her bed and howled with laughter. She tried to tell them to stop. She didn't feel well. The words wouldn't come. She couldn't speak. She woke up.

For a moment she was relieved to know it was

only a bad dream. Only for a second. Dr. Long, that was it! This afternoon was Dr. Long's day. Alison shook her head hard. Sometimes that made the bad things in her head go away. It didn't work. Alison stumbled out of bed into the bathroom. She felt as though she was going to be sick. She filled her hands with cold water and splashed it on her face. The sick feeling slowly passed. Still, the fact was she didn't feel well. She felt the way she always felt before another treatment. She couldn't get over being scared.

She collapsed on her bed, screaming, "Mama, Mama." She sobbed into her pillow.

"What is it, darling?" Her mother was there beside her in an instant. "Did you have another bad dream?" She held Alison's head in her lap, smoothing the hair out of her eyes.

"I don't want to see Dr. Long. I never want to see Dr. Long again. I hate him, I hate him, I hate him. He's always there waiting for me. I can get better without Dr. Long. Please, Mama, please. Let's stay home. I can't leave the doll hospital. We're always busy in the afternoons. Next week, Mama. I'll see Dr. Long next week. I promise. I'll be better by then. I know I will."

"My poor baby," her mother murmured. "We have to get you better, Alison, so you can spend all your time in the doll hospital. Dr. Long is helping to make you better."

"He's not, Mama. I'm getting worse. He puts me in that awful hospital. They make me sicker with their medicine and needles and machines. I never want to go back. It's not like the doll hospital. If it was like that, I wouldn't mind going back."

Her mother looked at her watch. "We have to go, Alison. I let you nap as long as I could. We'll put on something simple." She helped Alison to her feet first and into a blouse and skirt. She bent down to do her socks. "Slip into your loafers, Alison. We have to hurry."

There was a different woman in the waiting room, Alison noted. Her smile was about the same as the other woman's. "Good afternoon, Alison. Dr. Long is waiting for you and your mother."

"Up on the magic table, Alison," Dr. Long said in his cheerful voice. "How have you been?"

"Great," Alison lied. Maybe if she told him how great she was, he wouldn't notice that she wasn't.

Dr. Long listened to her chest for a long time. He looked into her eyes. Sometimes he forgot to do that. He looked deep into her throat. He wrapped a rubber bandage around her arm and squeezed a little ball. He pressed under her arms. Alison gave a little gasp. Dr. Long didn't say he was sorry. He patted her on the back and took her arm to help her down. She went across the room and onto the scales. The numbers flickered.

"You lost half a pound, Alison. What are you eating these days?"

Her mother answered for her. "She has been eating like a horse, Doctor, until the last day or two. She came to the kitchen for breakfast and lunch, didn't you, Alison?"

Alison nodded. Her mother's talk wouldn't make any difference. She already knew from Dr. Long's expression that things weren't so good. Now she waited, tense with anxiety, for him to tell her to go into the waiting room.

But he didn't. "Alison and I should have a talk, Mrs. Taggert," he said. "I'll give her back to you in a little while." It was Mama this time who excused herself and went outside to wait.

Dr. Long put Alison in his office chair and sat down on a stool in front of her. "We haven't had a good talk, Alison, since you were in the hospital. You are always in a hurry to get out of here with your doll. It makes me think you would rather not be here." He laughed a little bit.

Alison looked around the office for Nettie. She remembered that Nettie had stayed home. Her heart sank. She needed her friend Nettie now more than ever before. She didn't know what to say to Dr. Long. Nettie always gave her the answers when people wanted to talk seriously. She decided it would be best not to answer. She tried a smile, instead.

"Your dolls are pretty important to you, aren't they, Alison?"

Alison nodded. Why was Dr. Long talking to her about her dolls?

"You have your hospital now, your mother says. Christopher is the doctor and Nettie is the head nurse."

Alison nodded again. She wanted to leave. She felt it was safer out in the waiting room with the new woman she hadn't seen before. She liked her smile better than the last woman's smile.

"How many beds in your hospital?" Dr. Long wanted to know.

Alison counted on her fingers. "Nine," she answered. "We don't have many patients yet."

"It's good to be prepared. You can never tell what's going to happen. There might be an epidemic."

Alison nodded. She didn't know what he meant, but she wasn't about to ask. She liked it better when Dr. Long was the doctor, not someone trying to be her friend. That was a bad sign.

"I better go outside," she said. "I'm not feeling so well. I'll go out and wait for you to talk to my mother."

Dr. Long walked her out to the waiting room. "Miss Drago will take you to the lab for some samples, Alison. I think she has something for your friends in the doll hospital. We'll have another talk soon. Be sure to bring Nettie the next time. I want to talk to her, too."

When they came back from the lab, Miss Drago asked her how many friends she had in the doll hospital.

Alison counted again, not on her fingers this time, but in her mind: Nettie and Boodles and Denise and the twins and Grandpa Rabbit and maybe Christopher. "Seven, I guess," she said.

Miss Drago took a box from the desk drawer and opened it. Inside were hard candies of all different colors. "They are from England," she confided. "I ate one this morning, a strawberry one. It was the best I ever tasted."

Alison chose strawberry for Nettie, lemon for Grandpa Rabbit, grape for Boodles, two orange ones for the twins, a white one for Denise, green for Christopher. And for herself? Alison looked, then shook her head. "Thank you. That is fine. I don't feel like candy today. Maybe next time."

Chapter Twenty-Five

"It's my fault," her mother was saying. "I let her overdo it with that doll hospital. Some days she didn't even take her nap. I couldn't keep after her to follow the routine, Ted. It didn't seem fair. For the first time since she's been sick she had something that was her own."

Alison slumped in the corner behind the door. She was a She again.

"You must stop blaming yourself, Marty. Dr. Long has told her to do whatever she feels like doing. Her doll hospital didn't hurt her. What did Dr. Long say exactly today?"

"He said it isn't working, that's what he said. These couple of good weeks didn't have anything to do with the treatment. It was Alison's own determination and interest in her dolls that made the difference."

"Determination," that was a good one. She would get one more word and go back to bed. She didn't altogether understand what Mama and Dad were talking about. They sounded unhappy. But her head was spinning and nothing they said made too much sense.

"He wants to use the new drug," Mama said. "He's going to ask for it, just to have it ready. It may take some time for him to get it."

"We still have to give permission, is that it?" Dad asked.

"That's it. They have had some good results with children. He kept repeating there were no guarantees. It was almost as if he didn't believe in it himself."

"Guarantees," that was it. "Determination, guarantees, determination, guarantees," Alison repeated, making her way down the hall. She peeked into the hospital. Christopher had put a night-light into the wall. Everyone was asleep, even the twins. Mama was right. She *had* done something. She had made a doll hospital, and everyone there was well and happy. That was something, she told herself. Even if I can't look after myself, I can look after dolls and furries.

In the morning Alison told her mother that she wanted her breakfast tray. "Is that all right,

Mama? I feel sort of weak right now."

"Of course it's all right. I'll send Christopher in with a tray. We'll miss you, darling. Maybe we'll see you tomorrow morning."

Nettie made her report while Alison ate. "The twins slept through the night," she announced. "Grandpa Rabbit says they will be all right now. The first night is important. For a furry he knows a lot about babies."

"Rabbits have big families, Nettie. Why do you suppose he calls himself Grandpa?"

"Christopher, we need another patient," Nettie said as Christopher took the tray from Alison's bed. "Have you passed out the second announcement?"

Christopher shook his head. He was in a hurry. "Good-bye, Princess. I have to get ready for school. You look after things, Nettie."

"Wait a minute, Christopher. Could you distribute the announcements again this afternoon, please? I feel better when there is a patient in the hospital to look after." She remembered the words. "Oh, wait. What does 'determination' mean?"

"That means making up your mind you are going to do something. Nettie, for example, is a very determined doll."

"And me?" Alison asked.

"I think so," Christopher said. "You do get

discouraged once in a while, but it doesn't last long. I have to run. See you this afternoon."

"One more, please, 'guarantee.' "

"That means you are so certain something will happen or something will work that you will give people their money back if it doesn't. Good-bye again. I'm off."

"Did you hear that, Nettie? I picked up two new words for you last night."

"I heard. Christopher said you and I had determination. I'll tell you one thing, Boodles doesn't have any. He can't do the same thing two days in a row. 'Guarantee,' we don't have much use for that. Hospitals can't give guarantees, can they, Alison? We do the best we can, but that is all we can do. I mean, who would have given a guarantee on Looey the afternoon he came in?"

Nettie stopped chattering. Something was wrong. Alison was looking across the room, although there wasn't anything in particular to look at. "What's the matter, Alison? Did I say something wrong?"

"I think I have to go back to the hospital, Nettie, for some treatments. I don't want to go. Dr. Long told Mama and Dad — at least I think he did, I couldn't hear very well — there aren't any guarantees it will work. I am going to be sick forever."

"That's silly," Nettie said. "You never want to go until you get there, then we have a pretty good time. It's not so bad. We're used to it by now. Some of the nurses are neat."

"Yes, but this time they are going to give me something different. Experimental, maybe. I'm scared."

"Don't worry, Alison. Dr. Long is a good doctor, even if he doesn't speak to me. He knows who I am."

"He wants to talk to you, too, he says," Alison told Nettie. "He wants to have a good talk with you."

"He must have found out I was a head nurse now. That does make a difference."

Nettie and Alison were silent. Nettie slipped her hand into Alison's. She didn't know what to say. Finally, she spoke. "You know what, Alison? I have this feeling everything is going to be all right. Grandpa Rabbit says he gets a feeling in his bones before something good happens. I have the same feeling. You have a lot of friends now to pull you through, not just me. You have a hospital full of friends. That's pretty important. It should give you a lot of determination. That's better than a guarantee."

"And maybe before you go off," Nettie went on, "Christopher will find us another patient. What we need now is a sick girl doll we can cure. Then we will all know what to do. No more furries or babies for a while. Let their own folks look after them."

Alison scarcely heard all that Nettie said, but she nodded politely. She didn't feel well. She huddled up on her side, holding Nettie close. "Thank you, Nettie," she said.

Chapter Twenty-Six

Christopher delivered the special annouce-ment with the afternoon paper. The next day Alison and her friends waited impatiently for the phone to ring at four o'clock with a call for help. No one called. Day after day, it seemed, they sat in the hospital, with the door open, hardly talking, waiting for their next patient. Grandpa Rabbit told them funny stories, but only Boodles laughed.

At four-thirty, Alison slumped back in her bed, tired out and discouraged. Her mother brought her a glass of ginger ale with a curly plastic straw, and an oatmeal cookie. Alison took a sip, just enough to see the ginger ale make its way up the roller coaster straw. She nibbled at the cookie and put it back on the plate.

"What's the matter, Mama? There have to be some sick dolls where Christopher delivers his papers. He said lots of kids lived on his route."

"You did get three patients, Alison, don't forget that; four, if you count both twins. That was pretty good. If we wait, someone is bound to become ill or get hurt. Most dolls are pretty healthy. They have a soft life, looked after all the time by someone who loves them more than anything else in the whole, wide world. They don't have any reason to be sick, unless they have an accident."

"Maybe that's so, Mama, but what about me? I'm not a doll. I am looked after all the time and you love me. I never seem to get well."

"You have to be patient, Alison. This is a bad time for you, I realize. You are going to be healthy again, and your hospital will be filled with dolls and furries. We have to settle down and wait for it to happen. Shall I read you a story?"

Alison understood that she wasn't going to get well right away. Dr. Long hadn't told her she would. He was the one who knew. Every time she went to his office, Alison listened for him to promise her that, but he never did.

"No thanks," she sighed. "I like Grandpa Rabbit's stories better than the ones in books, even though they don't have any pictures."

Her mother wasn't paying attention. She was looking worried. "It's hard to stay in bed most of the time. It's what Dr. Long said you should do now. No more exertion for a while."

"I felt all right when I had a sick doll to look after," Alison complained. "It didn't cure me, maybe, but I felt better."

"Tomorrow may be your lucky day, darling. Sometimes I have a feeling in my bones, too — the way you say Nettie does — about something good happening. My bones tell me tomorrow will be different. Now I have to fix supper. Anything special for you?"

"I'm not hungry, Mama. Just a little bit, a real little bit, of whatever the rest of you are having."

After supper, Alison couldn't sleep. She was uncomfortable. The bottom sheet wrinkled up under her. The summer blanket on top of her weighed a ton. Her pillow wouldn't plump up because she had used it so much. She heard a couple of teenagers talking to Christopher outside. It was Perky and Diana. Christopher wouldn't tell Alison what Perky's real name was. They came down the street a couple of nights a week to talk to Christopher on the front steps. They giggled a lot. One night Alison thought she smelled cigarette smoke. She didn't ask Christopher about it. He wouldn't even tell her what they talked about. He got sort of red in the face and said, "Nothing in particular."

Nettie told her she listened, too. She put her box under the window and stuck her head up to the window. "All teenagers are silly," she told Alison.

Alison heard the familiar hum of voices from the living room. She might as well go down the hall to hear what was going on. She hadn't listened for a long time, it seemed. She was afraid now of hearing something she didn't want to hear. She had a feeling it probably didn't matter anymore what she heard. She might catch a new word for Nettie, that was all.

"I'll meet you at the doctor's at three-thirty," Dad said. "Christopher will be home by then to baby-sit. We had better do what he says, Marty. We really don't have a choice any longer."

"Ted, what if he's wrong? I couldn't live with myself, and maybe not with you. I couldn't. I would keep telling myself I had signed my daughter away."

"Marty, we have to. You are with her all the time. You can see she is wearing out. The count is going down. If it goes down much more, nothing is going to work."

"He wants to talk to her, Ted. That seems too cruel to me. I don't think we should permit it. What is he going to say to an eight-year-old girl?

Tell me, what is he going to say?"

"We will ask him tomorrow, Marty. Please, no tears tonight. It will be all right. I'm absolutely certain it will be all right."

Mama did start to cry. It was the end of the talk. What did they mean, Alison wondered, that Dr. Long wanted to talk to her, too. He had told her that, but he didn't make it sound important. Alison supposed he wanted to talk about the doll hospital.

Back in bed, she didn't think much about what she had heard. Alison had a feeling of her own, not in her bones like Nettie and Mama, just a feeling that nothing mattered much anymore. After a while, when you were sick all the time, you couldn't even remember what it was like to be well. Nothing changed. Nothing mattered.

Her mother was gone before she awoke from her nap. Christopher was sitting at Dad's desk, doing homework. "Hi, Christopher," Alison said in a thick voice. "What are you doing?"

"I'm writing a paper for history. It's about the Pilgrims again. Every year I have to write about the Pilgrims."

"Who are they?" Alison didn't really care, but she thought she ought to ask if Christopher was fed up with them.

"The people who came over here from England three hundred and fifty years ago and started a settlement. They wanted to be free to worship as they chose. They couldn't do that in England. Anyway, they had a big meal and invited some Indians. That was the first Thanksgiving. I'll save this paper. I'll use it again next year when they tell us to write about the Pilgrims."

It sounded dull to Alison. "Do you think you will pick up a patient when you deliver today, Christopher?"

"I sure hope so. We're getting close to flu season. We may have a patient or two soon. What do you want, a doll or a furry?"

"Nettie wants a doll. I did, too, a while back. Now I don't care. Just a patient. Someone who needs attention. Someone we can make better."

Chapter Twenty-Seven

"Her name is MiMi," her mother said. "She has a capital M in the middle of her name. That makes her very fancy, Dr. Long says."

Alison clutched the beautiful redheaded doll to her breast. She had never seen such a doll. Denise was beautiful and certainly should have won the prize in Paris, because Denise had style, Mama said, and sometimes style was better than beauty. And Nettie was beautiful, too, in her friendly-bossy way. Nettie had character, that's what Christopher said last year when he wrote a story about Nettie the Doll for his English class. And that was even before Nettie had begun talking to him.

MiMi was something else. Alison felt a twinge

of disloyalty as she regarded the tall redheaded doll in her black tights and leotard. Her red hair was cut close to her pale face with startling green eyes. Alison was certain there had never been a doll like MiMi.

Dr. Long's name echoed in her head. "Dr. Long," was that what Mama had said? "My Dr. Long?" she asked. "How does he know MiMi?"

"Certainly, your Dr. Long, darling. Dad and I went to talk to him this afternoon. While we were there one of Dr. Long's patients brought MiMi in. Dr. Long is MiMi's doctor, too."

"What's the matter with MiMi?" Alison asked. "She's a little pale and probably underweight. She looks like a dancer; she doesn't look sick."

"She is sick," her mother said. "She won't eat. She cries a lot. She is getting worse, Dr. Long says, and the girl she lives with can't look after her. She needs a hospital. Dr. Long recommended your hospital, Alison. He said it was the only one he knew of that specialized in dolls. He was sure if you and Nettie were in charge, it had to be very good. MiMi is your patient now."

"What will Nettie and Denise say?" Alison wondered. "Nettie can be pretty jealous. What if Denise is jealous, too?"

"French dolls would never be jealous," her mother said. "They are convinced they are the most beautiful dolls in the world. As for Nettie, well, Nettie is the head nurse. This is a professional case for Nettie, not a family affair."

"Does she talk, Mama?"

"She didn't say a word to us. I think she talked to Dr. Long. You can ask him next week."

"Next week?" It seemed to Alison that she had been to see Dr. Long only yesterday. "What for, Mama? I just had a check-up."

"He wants to see MiMi, too. And Nettie. He's worried about MiMi. Head Nurse Nettie will have to keep track of her progress. Dr. Long sent her pills along."

Alison's mother reached in her purse. She brought out a little brown container with a white paper taped around it. It looked just like the ones that held Alison's different pills. Her mother shook some green-and-yellow capsules into her hand. "One of these in the morning, it says here, and another at bedtime until they are gone. Tell Head Nurse Nettie that MiMi has to take naps morning and afternoon. Boodles may walk with her twice a day to the door and back. She can have stories anytime. Maybe MiMi can learn a little French while she is there. No sewing lessons until later."

"I'll take her into the hospital now. Give me the pills. Nettie has a medicine cabinet she keeps things in."

Alison hurried into the doll hospital with MiMi. "Look," she almost shouted. "We have a patient. Her name is MiMi with a big M in the middle, and she has been sick for a long time."

Alison sat down by the door. She introduced MiMi first to Nettie, who came across the room to shake hands. Alison noticed that Nettie didn't smile. Next was Denise, who said, "*Enchantée*, MiMi. You must be French." Boodles lifted his head to say, "How are you doing, MiMi? Glad to see you." The twins were asleep and didn't say anything. Grandpa Rabbit said, "MiMi, eh? I remember I knew a MiMi once, a country rabbit, I think. Only she had a little M in the middle. What is your last name, Miss?"

"Bookin, MiMi Bookin," the redheaded doll replied. "That is my stage name. It is what I prefer to use. I am very pleased to meet all of you. I will try not to be a bother while I am here."

"Stage name?" exclaimed Christopher who had just come in to tell Alison and the staff he was headed off on his paper route. "You are an actress?"

MiMi Bookin looked at Christopher. She didn't answer right away. Then she replied. "Yes. And who are you?"

"I am Christopher Taggert, the resident doll doctor. My mother says you are sick. Dr. Long is your regular doctor, I believe?"

"Yes. He told me you would be in charge of my case. He says you have a very fine hospital."

"What is wrong with you?" Christopher asked. "Did Dr. Long tell you?"

"Oh, yes, it is some kind of special anemia. I brought my pills with me."

"That is good," Christopher said. "Head Nurse Nettie is in charge of pills. Tell me, where were you an actress?"

"On the stage, of course, and on television, where you may have seen me. I was the star of the Dollhouse Players."

"Yes, you were, of course you were," Grandpa Rabbit interrupted. "I remember that show. I thought you looked familiar. I saw you many times. You *are* a star, Miss Bookin."

"I am not a star now," MiMi said. "I have been ill for many months and I do not have the strength to act. Dr. Long is very worried. Nothing he has done has worked. I am still worn out. I have dizzy spells. I have lost my appetite. The doctor has given me this new drug. It is experimental. He thinks it will work."

Alison could hardly think. A real television star in her hospital. MiMi Bookin! Grandpa Rabbit had actually seen her. She was no ordinary patient. She even had her own pills. They would have to look after her with great care. "Do you want to be an actress again?" she asked.

"I no longer know what I want," MiMi Bookin said. "Sometimes I simply don't care. More than anything right now, I want to get well. Then I will decide."

Chapter Twenty-Eight

"What time do you take your pill, Miss Bookin?" Nettie wanted to know. "Alison can tell time," she said proudly. "She will tell me when it is pill time and I will give it to you. That's how it works here. I keep your pills in my medicine cabinet over there. I have never seen pills like these before."

"They are very special new pills. Dr. Long said they were experimental and might make me sick before they make me better. I am starting on them this evening. After that, one in the morning and one at bedtime until they are gone."

"Well, he sent you to the right place," Nettie declared. "We are very good at curing patients, aren't we, Alison?"

Alison did not hear Head Nurse Nettie. She was watching MiMi Bookin with admiration. The redheaded doll was sitting on the hospital table, swinging her long legs and holding a mirror to her face while she combed her hair. She looked like the women in a magazine Alison's mother received every month in the letter box. She wondered if Nettie saw the actress the same way she did.

For the moment, Nettie didn't seem to care one way or another. MiMi Bookin was another patient to be looked after. Nettie had on the new blue-and-white-striped uniform Denise had made her from Dad's old shirt, and her white cap with a red cross on the front. She and Denise were preparing MiMi's bed.

When the bed was ready, Nettie announced it was bedtime. "Here is your gown," she told MiMi, handing her a white gown with ties in the back. "Denise will help you change. When you are in bed, I will bring you a pill. Alison will give you some water to swallow it down with."

MiMi Bookin looked down her nose at the gown. "I couldn't wear *that!*" she exclaimed. "I think I'll just sleep in what I have on whenever I go to bed. I generally don't go to bed until after midnight. Actresses are creatures of the night, you know."

Nettie looked at Alison. "What is she talking about?"

Alison snapped to attention. "I think she means that actresses work at night and go to bed whenever they want to."

"She is not an actress here," Nettie said. "She is a patient. They go to bed at eight o'clock when Alison turns the lights out. Those are hospital rules, Miss Bookin. You also have to wear the gown."

"But I am a special patient," MiMi Bookin argued. "Special patients can dress as they please.

They go to bed when they want to."

"There are no special patients in this doll hospital. Isn't that right, Denise?"

Poor Denise didn't know what to say. She tried to find an answer that would satisfy both Nettie and MiMi. "Well," she began.

Alison realized she had to step in. She was the director of the hospital. It had been a long afternoon and evening, and she was exhausted. She had better solve the dispute quickly and get to her own bed.

"Nettie is the head nurse, MiMi," she told the actress. "All of us have to do what she says. When I am sick, which is most of the time, Nettie is in charge of me, too. Anyway, the clothes you have on will be uncomfortable to sleep in. Do you usually sleep in tights and a leotard?"

"No. I have a drawer full of silk nightgowns and pajamas. I didn't have a chance to bring them with me."

"Ah," Denise said. "I have the answer. Tomorrow I will make you some beautiful French nightgowns. If you are not sick from your pills, Nettie will allow you to wear them during the day. Isn't that so, Nettie?"

"I suppose it will be all right. But now it is a hospital gown and lights out."

MiMi Bookin didn't fight any longer. She just slid off the table and let Denise help her change.

Then she climbed into bed and told Nettie to bring her the pill.

Alison used up her last bit of strength to bring a cup of water from the bathroom. Nettie popped in the pill, and Alison held the cup to MiMi's mouth. She smoothed MiMi's hair and smiled at her. "Good-night, MiMi. We are glad you are here. You will be all right soon. We are going to look after you."

As she turned off the light and went out the door, she heard Grandpa Rabbit begin to tell MiMi Bookin the story about the time he worked for the circus.

The actress was very sick for days. Sometimes she rolled from one side of her box to the other, moaning, saying things that didn't make any sense. Other times she passed into a deep sleep from which no one could awaken her. For a while she was delirious. She had a fever that went up rapidly and came down just as rapidly. It was very difficult to make her take her pill.

Christopher checked up on her before he went to school and as soon as he came home from school. "It is beyond me," he said. "MiMi is really Dr. Long's patient. I'll ask Mama if I should call him."

"No, Christopher," Alison said. "We won't call him. When Dr. Long sent us MiMi Bookin, he must have known the medicine would make her sick like this. He told her it might, anyway. We will wait and see. There are only six pills left."

Alison wasn't feeling that great, either. She could hardly drag herself into the doll hospital. Each day she spent more time in her own bed. There wasn't much she could do for MiMi. It was Head Nurse Nettie's case now. And Christopher's. Alison just wanted to lie in bed and not think about anything. What went on in the doll hospital was beyond her now.

Nettie and Denise came to visit and make their report. Grandpa Rabbit sat beside her and told her story after story which she didn't actually listen to. The sound was nice. She scratched the old rabbit's ears while he spoke. Poor Boodles kept asking if there was anything he could do. Alison shook her head. "No thanks, Boodles." She reached down and pulled Boodles up on the bed to hug him. Boodles wagged his tail. As soon as Alison drifted off, Boodles closed his eyes and went to sleep, too.

Days passed without a visit to the hospital. One afternoon, Nettie came in. "Shut your eyes, Alison. We have a surprise for you."

Alison's eyes were already closed. "Okay," she said. She felt someone climb up on the bed, then someone else. Then another, and still another. She heard some giggles.

"Open your eyes, Alison," Nettie commanded.

Lined up across the foot of the bed was the hospital staff, plus the twins, who were poking fingers into each other's eyes, and the famous actress MiMi Bookin in blue-and-gold beach pajamas. She smiled at Alison.

"MiMi Bookin is cured," Nettie announced. "Our first really serious case — except for that silly Looey — and we pulled her through. We know what we are doing. Christopher said he was proud of us."

"That's wonderful," Alison heard herself saying. "I am proud of you, too. I haven't been

much help. I just feel tired all the time."

"I know how you feel," MiMi said. "I felt the same way for, oh, such a long time. The pills cured me. I feel like my old self again."

"Are you going home now?" Alison asked. She didn't want MiMi Bookin to leave right away.

"No," the actress answered. "I am going to help the staff make you well. And I have begun my French lessons from Denise. Then I want to learn to sew. It is important for an actress to know these things. I think I will stay here for a good while."

Alison was relieved. She wasn't able to say so at the moment. "That's good," she mumbled. "I have to sleep now. Then we'll talk about it."

Chapter Twenty-Nine

Alison was dimly aware that someone was sitting on her bed. She was lying on her side facing the wall. The room was in shadows. It wasn't Mama or Christopher sitting there, she was certain. It might be Dad, except that he wasn't so heavy. "Dad?" she murmured. "Is that you, Dad?"

"It's not your dad, Alison. It's someone else," a man's voice said. "Do you want to guess?"

Her head was fuzzy, yet the voice sounded familiar to Alison. And the smell, some kind of lotion, that was familiar, too. It was a doctor's smell.

"Dr. Long," she said, rolling over on her back

and opening her eyes. "What are you doing here?"

"I dropped by to check on my patient," the voice said. "Did I wake you up?"

"I guess not. What did you want to see me for? I'm all right, just a little tired."

Dr. Long laughed. "Not you, Alison. I came to see my other patient, MiMi Bookin. I have just been in your hospital. It is quite a place."

Alison forced herself to sit up and pay attention. She shook her head to make it work better. She reached over for the glass of water. Dr. Long handed it to her.

"MiMi is cured. She came in to visit this afternoon with the staff. She said she felt fine. You aren't going to take her away, are you? She still needs some rehabilitation."

"No, I'm not going to take her away. As a matter of fact, MiMi and I talked about that. She thinks she might stay here forever. She never had any close friends until now. She could put on shows for your patients. MiMi is a good impersonator."

Alison was forcing herself to follow what Dr. Long was saying. "Imperso-what?" she asked.

" 'Impersonator.' " That's an actress or actor who pretends to be someone else, usually a famous person, and acts just like them. Just now

MiMi did an impersonation of Nettie. It even made Nettie laugh."

"I wish I had seen it," Alison said. "I have trouble getting out of bed now. I must have overdone it in the doll hospital. I am going to be a good girl from now on, Dr. Long, I promise. I'll stay here in bed for a couple of days until I get my strength back. Then I'll start being healthy again. The treatment was working for a while. I felt good."

"I know that, Alison." Dr. Long was serious now. "But I believe it wasn't the treatment that made you feel better. It was the doll hospital. You were so busy you forgot about yourself for a while. You were using your reserve strength. But you used it up, and now you are back in bed."

Alison felt cold and sick inside. It seemed she had been through this so many times before. She already knew what came next. "No," she almost shouted. "It won't come back. I won't let it. I'm just tired, that's all. I'm just tired."

"Try to listen to me, Alison. I have something important to say. I have talked with your mother and father. I told them I would have to talk to you because you are the patient. I like to be honest with my patients. You are big enough to understand, Alison. You run a hospital. You couldn't manage that unless you understood what sickness is."

"I'm not going back, Dr. Long. I don't care about the pain. It will go away. It always does. I'll rest here and the pills will make it go away."

"Alison, it's not going to go away. We have to chase it away. You have a bad disease. You have had it for over two years. The things we have done so far only work for a little while. I think we should try to get rid of it once and for all. Let's strike back, Alison."

"Strike back." Alison had been fearful about these words since she'd first heard them. Now she was terrified, though she wasn't sure what they meant.

"No," she said firmly and turned her back to Dr. Long. "I won't do it. I won't. I don't care what Mama and Dad and you say. I know more about being sick than you do. Please leave me be, Dr. Long. I want to go back to sleep."

Alison felt the weight lifted from her bed. The room grew dark again as Dr. Long shut the door behind him. She pulled her knees up under her, taking care not to push them into her sore side, and closed her mind to what had happened.

She had almost passed into a troubled sleep when she felt another weight on the bed. And another and another. Nothing very heavy. They were familiar weights this time. They were down at the end of her bed. She heard something that seemed far, far away.

"Psst, Alison, can Denise and I come up to your end?"

"Okay," Alison mumbled. "What do you want?"

"I'll tell you if you promise to listen. Will you listen?"

"Okay, I promise. But I'm awfully sleepy. Who's there with you?"

"Grandpa Rabbit, Boodles, and MiMi Bookin. The twins are asleep. They said their first words today."

"That's good," Alison managed to say.

"Listen, Alison," Nettie spoke right in her ear. "We have been talking to Dr. Long. He says he is pretty sure he can make you better. He just got this experimental drug, sort of like the pills he gave MiMi Bookin. He thinks it can make you well forever. How about that, Alison?"

"Go away, Nettie. No more hospitals. I can't, Nettie. I'll be fine if I stay here and rest. I know I will."

"Alison," Nettie spoke sharply. "That is not so. You haven't been in our hospital for three days. We need you. Christopher had to turn down two cases, real good cases, he said."

"No, let me sleep."

"I can't, Alison. You see, Dr. Long says we

can all go to the hospital to look after you with the regular nurses. He promised us. You go, we go. That's how it is."

Alison turned over again. "You can stay in the room with me? On my bed? The nurses won't allow that. When you went with me the other times, Nettie, they put you on a bureau across the room where you couldn't get down. I couldn't hear you from there. All we could do was wave to each other."

"Do you want to talk to Dr. Long?"

"Yes. I don't believe it."

"Come in, Dr. Long," Nettie shouted.

Dr. Long appeared in the doorway.

"Is what Nettie says true, Dr. Long?"

"Yes."

Alison drew a deep breath. She wanted to have it all straight. "This is the same drug MiMi Bookin took?"

"It's like that drug, Alison. You don't have the same sickness MiMi had. This drug is more powerful. Hers was doll medicine. It was in a pill."

"You mean mine's not? Mine's in those bottles and tubes and bags you hang over my bed?"

"Yes, that's what I mean, Alison. Just like before, but the medicine is different."

"Will it make me sick, like MiMi was sick?"

"Yes. It will make you sick for a couple of days. You'll have chills and be delirous maybe.

Maybe you'll throw up. It won't be easy, Alison, I'll be honest with you. We're going to need help. That's why I said your friends can go with you. They know what to do. They will help look after you."

"The nurses will throw them out. Some of them are nice, but they are strict, too."

"I won't let them. Well, Alison, what do you say? Will you do it?"

Dr. Long's voice was drifting away. Alison was so tired. "I suppose so," she whispered.

"Your friends are ready if you are, Alison." Dr. Long reached down to the bed and picked her up. "Let's start now," he said and carried her down the hall.

Chapter Thirty

Alison couldn't be sure, but it looked like an ambulance waiting for her at the end of the walk. And a man and a woman who took her from Dr. Long to a bed inside and put a strap around her. She had been in an ambulance once before. She didn't remember that very well, either. She was as confused then as she was now.

The hospital seemed to be like it always was. A piece of tape covered something sticking in her arm and a tube led up to a plastic bag. Nurses bustled around, and Mama and Dad were there with fuzzy faces that came and went away and came back again.

"Try to take deep breaths, Alison," a strange voice said. "Keep taking deep breaths."

There was a light in the room like the sun when a cloud passed over it. Dr. Long was at the foot of her bed; she could see him whenever she opened her eyes. He had a big basket in his hand. He was taking things out of the basket and putting them at the bottom of her bed. She was so far away she couldn't see what they were clearly.

"Dr. Long," she made herself whisper, "What are you doing?"

Dr. Long spoke to what he had in his hand. Alison couldn't hear. Something climbed up beside her. "It's only us, Alison," a familiar voice said. "We're right here to look after you. Go to sleep now. They are going to start the medicine. It's better if you are asleep."

Alison could feel Nettie take her hand and hold it in her lap. Nettie had her nurse's apron on. Alison let herself fall into the deep darkness of sleep.

Strange dreams, some good and some bad, appeared to Alison. She was hot, then cold. Then hot. The walls of her room turned into flaming colors. They pressed toward her. Then moved away. Her head throbbed as it had never throbbed before. Denise — was it Denise? — she couldn't be sure — laid cool cloths across her brow. Other times Nettie and Denise were holding a little bowl under her chin when she was about to throw up. Christopher and Dr. Long whispered softly in the corner of her room like ghosts in their white coats.

When the room that spun around her was dark, Alison could hear singing. When the spinning stopped for a moment, she recognized Grandpa Rabbit and MiMi Bookin and the twins. When she could stop the ringing in her ears, the sounds became little nursery songs. The twins had learned to sing! MiMi had taught them to sing. Then the delirium took over and the sounds faded into the buzzing that filled the room.

The confusion of light and shadows and movements and sounds passed over her as she lay there, helpless. Eyes squeezed closed against the delirium, she did the only thing she could. She breathed deeply, one-two-three, one-two-three.

She heard a voice. She understood the words. She felt the tug on her arm. The voice said, "That's it, Alison. You have all the medicine you need in you. Now we have to keep track of it."

She tried to open her eyes. The lids were stuck shut. "A washcloth, Nettie," she managed to say. "My eyelids are stuck." She heard Denise and Nettie talking. She felt a warm cloth on her face. She opened her eyes. She could see. There was no blurry light overhead. The room was filled with sunshine. Dr. Long was sitting beside her bed. A nurse she thought she recognized stood behind him. Nettie and Denise were at her pillow. At the foot of her bed, smiling and crying at the same time was Mama. Dad had his arm around her. Where was Christopher? He wasn't in the room.

"Christopher," she croaked. "Where is Christopher?"

"He's sleeping, Alison," Dr. Long said. His voice wasn't a long way off. "Your brother didn't leave the room for five days. Neither did your friends."

Alison smiled and shut her eyes. She was exhausted, but she didn't feel bad. "Thank you all," she said.

The days passed. Alison could feel her strength coming back. Her mind could focus on her room and her parents and Dr. Long and her friends from the doll hospital.

She began to eat. The Jell-O made her empty stomach gurgle. Amy and Becky were lying next to her, chattering away. They giggled at the gurgle and made sounds like the ones in Alison's stomach.

"Shhh," said Nettie. "You kids keep that up and I'll chase you down to the end of the bed."

On the day that Alison sat up for the first time, MiMi Bookin did her impersonating act. She put on Nettie's apron and puckered her lips and looked serious while she walked back and forth, tidying things up and fussing at Boodles. Then she put on Grandpa Rabbit's jacket and picked up the twins. She told them a silly story that got all tangled up in the middle. Nettie and Alison howled with laughter. Finally, MiMi Bookin put on eye shadow and a handkerchief around her shoulders. She took a straw and pretended it was a cigarette. She put her head back and sang a song in French in Denise's husky voice. Poor Denise blinked and hid her face in her hands.

That evening, Alison dared to ask Dr. Long when she was going home. "I feel pretty good. I have to get back to my own hospital."

"Not right away, Alison. We have to keep track of you day by day for a while. We have to keep making tests until we are certain the medicine did its job. It's better for you to stay here than it is for you to go home and keep coming back. From now on you can do practically what you want. Try to stay out of the way of patients who are wobbly on their feet."

Boodles declared he was in charge of rehabilitation. He tied the belt from Alison's bathrobe to his collar and led her up and down the halls to the sunroom at the end. She talked to the patients there. When they wanted to see her friends, she borrowed a laundry basket and wheeled them down. The twins stood on

Grandpa Rabbit's shoulders, shouting, "Hi," at everyone they saw.

Then Nettie took charge the way she usually did. "Alison is my patient," she explained. "My staff and I pulled her through a very serious illness. She was very sick from an experimental drug. Alison has a lot of determination so she got well. Soon we are going back to our own hospital. We have our own patients there."

One afternoon MiMi Bookin put on a show for a crowd of patients and nurses in the sunroom. They cheered when MiMi finished the show in a top hat doing her famous tap dance.

In the evening Alison went with Grandpa Rabbit to the rooms of patients who weren't able to get out of bed. He told them stories that made them smile. They always asked him to return whenever he could.

Christopher came by every afternoon after school. "I have been collecting the names of patients for the doll hospital," he told Alison one afternoon. "I have seven signed up now; two are serious cases. I am going to ask Dr. Long again when we can expect you back." He poked under Alison's chin. She didn't jump. He tried to lift her from the chair and groaned, "You weigh as much as an elephant."

That evening Dr. Long came into her room with Mama and Dad. He was smiling. He was wearing a ski jacket and boots instead of his white coat. "It's time for you and me to get out of here, Alison. You may check out tomorrow morning. I'm checking out right now to go skiing up in Vermont. We both need a vacation from here, don't we?"

"Tomorrow!" Nettie shouted. "Did you hear that, Denise? My patient is cured; is she Dr. Long?"

"I believe so, yes," Dr. Long said. "All her tests are negative. That means we have chased it away, Alison. I think it's gone for good. My friends in Boston agree. You may go back to school after Christmas."

He paused for a minute. "She's the bravest patient I ever had," he told Mama and Dad. "You can be very proud of her. As for Nettie and her staff, we couldn't have done this without them. Wait here a minute."

Dr. Long came back into the room with an old black bag. "This is for you and the doll hospital, Dr. Taggert. It was my first bag. Before that it was my father's. You'll find it useful in the doll hospital. Oh, yes, one more thing, I almost forgot."

Two nurses and two patients from the sunroom came in with a large box in a wide, blue ribbon. They handed it to Alison. She made out the words in the card, "Good luck, Alison."

Nettie couldn't wait. She grabbed the end of the ribbon and pulled. "See what's inside, Alison. Quick!"

Alison peeped inside. "Are you sure, Nettie? You really want to know?"

"Yes, yes, of course I do. Let us see."

"You won't be sorry, Nettie, you promise? You do want to see what's inside?"

"Yes. Don't tease me, Alison. We all want to see," Nettie said.

"Okay, then." Alison took a white hospital coat from the box. It had a stethoscope and a little wristwatch attached to it. A name tag was pinned on the front. The name tag read DR. NETTIE.

"Well," said Nettie. "It's about time. I told you I would be a doctor, Alison."

"Oh, Nettie," Alison laughed, holding the doll close to her, "don't ever change. I couldn't love you if you changed."

About the Author

JAMES DUFFY was born in Elkton, Maryland, and received his Ph.D. from Harvard University. He is the author of *The Revolt of the Teddy Bears* (Crown Publishers) and a YA novel called *Missing* (Scribners). *The Doll Hospital* is his first book with Scholastic Hardcover. Mr. Duffy now lives in Arlington, Massachusetts.

APPLE®PAPERBACKS

Pick an Apple and Polish Off Some Great Reading!